# Cut Me In

## by Jack Karney

Black Gat Books • Eureka California

CUT ME IN

Published by Black Gat Books
A division of Stark House Press
1315 H Street
Eureka, CA 95501, USA
griffinskye3@sbcglobal.net
www.starkhousepress.com

Originally published in paperback by Pyramid Books, New York,
and copyright © 1959 by Almat Publishing Corp.



ISBN-13: 978-1-951473-18-1

Book design by Jeff Vorzimmer, ¡caliente!design, Austin, Texas
Proofreading by Bill Kelly
Cover art by Ernest Chiriacka

PUBLISHER'S NOTE:
This is a work of fiction. Names, characters, places and incidents
are either the products of the author's imagination or used
fictionally, and any resemblance to actual persons, living or dead,
events or locales, is entirely coincidental.



First Stark House Press/Black Gat Edition: December 2020

# One

Coley lay at the base of the tree, his hands clutching his right side as if to stop his life blood flowing from the bullet hole. Breathing heavily, he pushed himself up and staggered a few steps into the black void of the woods. When the pain became agony, he toppled over, first his knees, then the rest of him. The grass was alive with buzzing insects and furtive rustlings underfoot.

Mom, I'm cold, put the blanket over me. Mille? Where's Mille? I love you, darling, I love you.

He heard voices in front of him, lifted his head fearfully. Now the voices were behind him, around him, in his head. The killers had him surrounded and soon they'd catch up to him and put a gun muzzle against the back of his head and blow him out of this world.

If he didn't die first ...

He saw the figure, vague and black, moving stealthily yards away. Coley lay rigidly, feeling desperate and trapped, breathing again only when the figure had vanished. Coley held up his hands, the palms wet and black with blood. Hot nausea swept over him.

Mille, I love you, honest to God and hope to die.

Coley laughed harshly. He was going to die. He knew that. With a wrenching desolation, he thought, I'll never hold my Mille in my arms again, never ...

Coley tried to get up, failed. It began to drizzle, a cold wet rain that penetrated through to the skin. Coley closed his eyes, sobbed. That day he'd met Mille it had been raining too.

The early April rain was coming down as if the sky had broken wide open. Wearing a raincoat, his police cap safe and dry with the rest of his clothing in the bag he carried, Coley stood in the Armory doorway, looking for a cab. From inside the Armory came the jubilant voices of happy cops and their families celebrating appointments to a job that started at four thousand dollars a year and in three years rose to five thousand three hundred fifteen dollars a year. Then there was the extra loot, a hundred and twenty-five dollars for uniforms, payable at the end of a nine-month probationary period, two hours of overtime pay every forty-two hour week.

An empty taxi rolled down the street, rain water spraying out from under the wheels. Coley whistled and the hackie rolled the taxi to a stop.

As Coley stepped out from the Armory entrance, he muttered, "Just like a hackie, out in the middle of the gutter where you gotta swim your way across."

He stepped into a puddle, swore at the driver, yanked open the door and, head down, stepped into the cab. The meeting of skulls was more surprising than painful.

Coley clasped his forehead, "For cryin' out loud. What the hell you—"

He looked into soft blue eyes. The blonde hair stuck wetly against the side of her face and the mascara was a black smear under each eye but she was so beautiful the breath came whistling out of his teeth.

She sat down. "I'm sorry, but I'm half-drowned and I just can't go out there again."

Still undecided, Coley stared at the thinly-built man with a wisp of a mustache coming after her into the cab.

The man cried, "You've got your nerve, mister. This is our cab. We hailed it first. You'll have to get out and get another."

Coley's mind had been made up for him. Plunking

himself down alongside the girl, he pulled closed his door. "Mister," he said, "you got big rocks in your head."

Coley was glad the raincoat covered his uniform. A probationary patrolman could not afford the luxury of a hassle with John Q. Public.

The man began to splutter but the blonde said, "Come in out of the rain, Michael. We can share the cab."

The rain glistened on her bare shoulders and arms. A drop ran down her nose. She pawed at it, laughed as if enjoying it all.

The man closed his door but, refusing to sit down, said to the hackie, "Will you tell this person to get out?"

The hackie, a scrawny-necked man wearing a big sloppy hat that came down around his ears, didn't bother to turn around. "Make ya minds up, fellers. I gotta make a livin'. My wife and kids can't live on what I make on runnin' time. We gotta roll."

The man sat down on the edge of the seat. The girl moved to make room, only to find Coley's raincoat against her legs.

She said, "How silly of me not to take a wrap."

Coley said, "I'm going to Rivington Street. If I can drop you off some place, I'd be a happy man."

She had a smile in her eyes. "We're going to Brooklyn. Is Rivington Street in Brooklyn?"

Coley grinned. "I wish it were so I could go all the way with you. Looks like you'll have to drop me off before you cross the Williamsburg Bridge."

The man said, "All right, cabby."

The hackie sang, "Is everybody happy?"

Watching the girl run her fingers over her wet arm, Coley said, "The hackie asked you a question."

She looked bewildered. "He did? Oh, it's all right."

The taxi turned the corner. Coley said, "Your father is still sore."

She gave Coley a quick look out of narrowed eyes as the man cried, "I am not her father."

Coley said quickly, "I'm sorry. Just trying to make conversation. You smell real good."

She ignored him. "Michael, will you be up at Cangro's tomorrow? We're showing a cute fall number. You should see it."

Coley leaned back in his seat, listened to them for a while as he watched the rain slapping hard against the window. Outside it was black. Turning halfway in his seat, he studied her profile. A drop of rain glistened like a tear on her cheek and he had an urge to wipe it away. He was looking at the bulge made by the white taffeta over her breasts when she turned and caught his eye. Coley stared back at her and when the warm flush spread over her face he knew she had read what was in his eyes.

Coley smiled. "I never could keep a secret."

The man called Michael said, "Is anything wrong, Mille, darling?"

"No," she said. "Nothing. Aren't we near the bridge yet?"

Coley said, "Just a couple more blocks."

The man said, "Hurry it up, cabbie."

Coley laughed. "Keep it up, Mike, and so help me, I'll ride all the way to Brooklyn with you and your wife."

Michael was annoyed. "She is not my wife."

The girl said to Coley, "I'm sorry we inconvenienced you."

Coley shrugged. "You didn't. Hell, I could ride around with you the rest of the night, rain or shine."

That didn't offend her. "I'm afraid that's the bridge up ahead."

Coley leaned nearer the hackie's ear. "Stop on the next corner."

The rain had stopped quite abruptly and Delancey Street was crowded with people strolling up and down the wet, sloppy street.

The meter read one-fifty. Coley held out two dollars to the hackie.

Michael said, "This is my cab and you don't have to do that."

Through the open partition, Coley dropped the two dollars into the hackie's lap. "I pay my own way," he said. He turned to the girl "Maybe I'll see you again."

"I doubt it," the girl said and to Coley she seemed very happy about it. "Please close the door."

Coley slammed the door hard. "Sure," he cried. "So long, Mille."

He watched the cab pull away and suddenly had a peculiar ache in the pit of his stomach, an empty kind of feeling, as if something sweet had gone out of his life. Coley turned away, laughing to himself. An eighty-buck a week cop—make it sixty after deductions—and he wanted to get acquainted with an expensive piece of bric-a-brac who probably spit at ten-thousand-dollar-a-year men.

It was hot, sticky.

His valise clasped between his legs, Coley took off his raincoat, folded it inside out, lay it across his arm.

Coley turned up Clinton Street. It was almost midnight and the streets were pitted with black puddles. Store lights cut brilliant blue-white squares on the wet pavement. The dress and shoe stores were getting a big play by the window shoppers. Tired of being pushed around by the people, and impatient to get home, Coley walked in the gutter. A car horn honked. Coley kept walking.

Rivington Street was darker, dirtier. Children kicked at a pile of garbage until there was no pile. Then they lined up on a sidewalk.

"Fox and the geese," they cried, "come out of y'den. Five and five is ten."

They scattered into hallways, one chasing the rest, trying desperately to tag somebody slower.

The girls were playing a game Coley had never seen before. Paired, they clapped hands, moved in half-circles, crying, "one, two, button your shoe, three, four, close the door ..." A girl of three sucked on her thumb, her dreamy eyes following the play, her lips moving with the chant.

"Maria," a heavy woman cried down from an open window. "It's after twelve."

"All right, all right," a dark girl answered. "When I finish the game."

On the next corner, a man on a wooden platform was making an eloquent speech. The American flag drooped limply to his right. A handful of people stood around him, and nobody seemed to be listening.

Coley saw the neighbors around his stoop and felt suddenly self-conscious, as if the blue uniform was a blazing neon sign.

"Coley? That you, Coley?"

His mother broke away from the people at the stoop and came toward him, a tall gray-haired woman, horn-rimmed glasses on her thin, hooked nose. The neighbors turned to look.

Coley straightened his shoulders. "Hello, Mom." He took her arm, protection against the staring eyes, moved with her to the stoop. People nodded, murmured hello, awe in their voices, respect in their manner for this tall, strong man who wore a blue uniform. The same people who used to smile and talk freely to him suddenly were dumbstruck.

Everybody but Mom.

Proudly she said, "Doesn't my Coley look good in his uniform?"

"I didn't even know," Mrs. Goldfarb said. "The first I hear."

"You didn't know?" Coley's mother was surprised. "You mean to stand there and tell me I didn't tell you my Coley was a cop?"

Mrs. Goldfarb lifted her shoulders, her eyes disturbed. "I shouldn't live to see my daughter get married, I didn't know."

"Now you know," Coley said, embarrassed. "Good night, everybody. Comin', Mom?"

Without waiting for her reply, he went into the dim hallway, took the wooden steps two at a time. He had his coat off and his gun and holster on the table by the time she came into the fourth-floor apartment.

There were tears in Mom's eyes and he couldn't understand it. Mom wasn't the crying type. Sure, once in a while she cried, like when they made their annual visit to the Holy Cross cemetery. As soon as she'd put the flowers on Pop's grave, the tears would flow like water. But why now?

Coley felt a vague unease. "Spit it out, Mom, whatever it is. Let's have it."

The cry came up from inside her. "Why didn't you tell me tonight was graduation? Did I have to hear it from Brody, the cop on the beat? Coley, are you ashamed of me?"

"Mom, you know better 'n that. I just didn't think you cared one way or the other."

Her voice was tight, the words thin and sharp. "What else does a mother live for except for the pleasure she gets out of her children? And what greater pleasure than to see her children move up to finer things. Public school, high school, college ..." The tears flowed freely now.

His mouth dry all of a sudden, he said. "You didn't get a helluva lot of pleasure out of me." He waved away her protest. "You never did get to see me graduate junior high. I got my diploma in the back room because you promised the teacher I'd never come back to school. In the back room like somebody's bastard kid."

She drew her hand across her face in a tired gesture. "You deserved nothing better, hitting the teacher."

"He hit me first." He laughed bitterly. "It's all water under the bridge."

"Why didn't you ask me to come see you graduate?"

His face was flat, emotionless. "There was nothing to see, Mom. Honest to God. A lot of men acting like kids, showing off to the people in the gallery. Exercises, wrestling around. Then to show how smart they could be without getting orders, a silent drill. A gang of grown men moving around like robots."

She looked up at him with a quiet level glance. "You didn't answer my question. Why didn't you ask me to come?"

Coley looked down at the linoleum, washed clean, glistening with wax. Through the wax he could see the brown flooring where the linoleum had worn through. He walked to the window, touched the green and brown cotton drapes.

"It's got a hole in it," he said. "You could use another pair."

The silence became oppressive, heavy.

He said, "The whole apartment could use a paint job. I could do it myself on my forty-eight hours off. Just a couple weeks ... What do you want me to say, Mom? I don't know why."

"Aren't you proud of your job?"

Coley looked out the window. A mist was falling over the red brick tenements. The lamppost in the middle of the street cast pale light in a circle of chalked gutter and sidewalk. He could read the large markings. 'Joanie loves Bill,' then a couple of obscene words and, almost out of view, a series of boxes numbered from one to eight. Potsy ...

"It's a job, Mom, like a million other jobs. It pays me a salary, the best I could get so I took it."

Coley turned suddenly to look at her. "If I hurt you, Mom, if what I did wasn't right ... you know I didn't mean it like that."

"You're bitter," she said. "Ever since Francine ..."

Coley moved to the bedroom door. "I've forgotten I had a wife called Francine. Do me a favor, Mom, don't remind me."

He pushed open the door, went inside and gently closed the door behind him. Yellow light from the apartment across the alley filtered through the cracked windowpane and lay across the face of a sleeping five-year-old boy. Coley smiled down on the child. Poor Billy, he seemed so tired, as if he'd had a rough day. Coley took the blanket rolled in a ball at the foot of the bed, covered the boy's bare legs, the left one firm and straight, the right bony and thin.

Every cripple has a rough day.

A sudden ache in his throat, Coley turned quickly to get out of the room. The metal brace lying on the chair hit against Coley's leg, clattered to the floor. In a split second the boy sat up in bed, one arm supporting him.

"Dad? That you, Dad? How'd you make out? Get any medals, huh, Dad?"

Coley sighed. "I would wake you, me and my clumsiness."

Billy felt hurt. "You said you'd wake me when you got home from the graduation and tell me all about it."

Coley flicked on the light. With his fists Billy rubbed the glare out of his eyes, then held up his arms to be lifted. Coley grasped the boy under the armpits, lifted him with a whoop, swung him around in a full circle before sitting down, the boy on his lap.

Coley said, "If I'd have won a paper medal or something, I'd have wakened you, but what's the sense in telling you your old man was a big flopperoo?"

Soft brown eyes shone in the electric light. "My old man ain't not a flopperoo. He didn't win, it's a frame." He ducked away as Coley tried to run his fingers through the brown curly hair. "Lemme see how you look in your whole uniform with the gun on the side, huh, Dad, please?"

"Tomorrow," Coley said gently, "And the day after that."

Eagerness slurred the boy's words. "Lemme try on y'hat, yeah, Dad? Just to see how I'm gonna look when I grow up to be a cop."

Coley squeezed the boy. "Thought you wanted to be a fireman? You better go back to sleep before Grandma hollers."

Despite the boy's protests, Coley swung him into bed, covered him. When Coley came into the kitchen, Mom was pouring coffee into a cup.

She sat the pot back on the stove. "The nurse from the visiting Service gave Billy his massage today. Says he's doing all right."

"A million massages and he'll still be a cripple."

"Polio can be beat."

"Not by a stinking massage twice a week. He needs special attention, whirlpool baths in a hospital so he can be wheeled to and from his treatments. Don't tell me what Doctor Morse said about Billy getting just as good treatment at home. It's a lot of bunk. In a hospital with somebody to watch over him to see that he gets his treatment and exercises, he's a got a chance. Here, at home, he's a kid with a brace moving around on crutches."

She toyed with her coffee cup. "You need money for special nurses and special care."

He nodded fiercely. "That I know. With money you don't have to hang around here. The treatment don't help, you can go off to Europe, Russia, any place they got a doctor who might help. All we can do is listen to Doctor Morse."

He went into his room and undressed. Under a newspaper on his dresser he found a cigarette and after lighting it, sat down on his bed.

Hell, why keep jumping on Mom? It isn't her fault.

It was nobody's fault, nobody you could knock down and kick around for doing a thing to the grandest kid in the world.

Mom crying ... But she had a habit of shoving barbs into his backside, hurting. Like that crack about Francine. Maybe he hadn't forgotten the woman he'd loved more than anything or anybody in the world. Somebody like Francine you didn't just push out of your mind. But that didn't mean he was bitter! Maybe at first, but two years is a long time.

What burned him up were the people who had big mouths at the wrong time. If they had told him before the car crash, maybe he could have patched things up. But they kept their damn secret and not until Francine had died behind the steering wheel did they tell him that the red-headed Polack who had died with her had been her sweetheart.

# Two

It was a warm day in August. Coley Walsh was on the day tour, eight-to-four, posts forty-one, forty-two and forty-three. Four months had passed since he'd been assigned to this precinct. During those four months he had worked the cycle six times: eight-to-four for one week, then forty-eight hours off, which brought him in to work on the four-to-twelve shift and, after another week plus forty-eight hours off, he did the midnight-to-eight tour. Eight-to-four, four-to-twelve, twelve-to-eight, a week at a time, on and on.

On the day tour everything is normal: eating, sleeping, bowel movements. The day tour is noisier, kids running around, the grinding sound of the trucks and buses rips your thoughts into shreds, splitting your head wide open inside. On the day tour more people get into fights, crap games, muggings in hallways, in the shadows of the bridge, in alleys. On the day tour there are more car accidents, more kids to chase off the backs of trucks and buses. You work harder on the day tour, yet somehow, crazy as it sounds, it is easier. For, as a rule, trouble encountered during the day isn't of a vicious nature—if you disregard the occasional stick-up, the exception that makes the rule.

At night, on the four-to-twelve and mostly on the twelve-to-eight, things are rough. Rape, impairing the morale of minors and incest flourish in this neighborhood. The fourteen-year-old girl, her eyes blinded with tears, scared to go home lest her mother find out she'd been pulled up onto a roof by six teen-agers, her body violated against her will. The old woman begging you to get her husband sent to Bellevue Hospital; every night he exposed himself to his four girls, banged them around when they refused to sleep with him.

Every night, sometimes two or three times within a couple hours, there are muggings. Crazy kids hopped up on loco weed, tired of gang fights, go out on mugging jobs. The older boys give themselves shots of heroin, mainliners, and do stick-ups. Of course, all the thieves aren't addicts in need of money to buy expensive drugs. Some of them need the money to eat and live.

Hoodlums or pink-faced boys with innocent eyes, they give you a hard time. And, at night, they come out to seek their prey.

An ambulance went by, its siren drowning out the Negro congregation singing in front of the store-church on the corner. Now the ambulance was gone and the singing was louder. He stopped to listen, and had difficulty understanding the words.

"Lift up your hands," they sang. "To the Lord, bless the Lord, bless the Lord. Lift up your hands. Thank ye, Lord, thank ye, Lord."

He walked around them. Regulations called for him to disperse crowds, or groups that might disturb the peace. The first day on this beat, Coley had made an attempt to shoo the singers back into the store but they had defied him. When he tried force, the leader, a light-skinned Negro with a hairline mustache, called upon the Lord to smite down the minion of the law who dared interfere with the worshippers.

Later, Sergeant Henry had smacked his lips, rolled his eyes. "Yeh, Walsh, I know, I know. Fact is we ain't had much luck getting them off the corner. I figured maybe you'd do better. Oh, well, let 'em sing their brains out. This religious worship thing is a ticklish situation. Lock 'em up and a dozen newspapers will make headlines against suppression of religion. But someday I'm gonna blow my stack ..."

Panels of sunlight lay long gold fingers across the dirty sidewalk. In the distance thunder rolled and the voice of the storm became a sullen howling in the distance. Noise, noise, noise. Cars and people and the sky.

Sometimes he hated it, and sometimes the noise of the city blended in a pleasant drone of sound.

In the next two hours, Coley was kept busy breaking up a crap game in an alley, hustling off his beat a man and woman whose obscene gestures and swear words were drawing a crowd. He listened to a woman who sobbed out a tale of how her husband had sold her to a madam in a disorderly house. He quieted a bearded giant, large gray eyes swollen with drink, who had heaved a stove down a flight of stairs.

A gang of kids passed. One tougher than the rest, said something obscene. Coley didn't have to catch him, he just reached out and the boy was in his hands, tall, thin, defiant.

"Hit me and my old man will sue the pants off you."

Staring down at the red-faced boy, Coley tried desperately to control the urge to roll his fist against the insolent mouth. The boy's friends stood at a distance, laughing, taunting, deriding. Coley thought, if I hit this kid, Captain Reardon will chew my ear off.

Abruptly Coley pushed the boy from him. "Get movin' or I'll ram your teeth down your throat."

Coley rocked from his heels to his toes. He wished he had his club. On the eight-to-four beat cops didn't have clubs. "You gonna walk?"

The boy glanced at his friends, took fresh courage. His look was a challenge. "This is a free country—"

Coley pulled the boy's head between his thighs, held it firmly. With the billy he'd yanked out of his hip pocket he rapped the boy smartly on the buttocks, first one then the other. The boy shrieked in agony, Coley stepped back, looked up at the boy's friends.

"You fellers like to feel this too?"

They backed away, fear and resentment in their faces. The boy picked himself up from the sidewalk. He stood there, both hands clasping his buttocks, the tears rolling down his cheeks.

"You coulda killed me," he sobbed. "You coulda killed me."

"Keep movin' now," Coley waved to the gathering crowd, "the show's over. You," he pointed the billy at the boy, "scram!"

The boy limped away. At a distance, he turned, grasped his genitals. "This for you, you lousy ..." The gang joined him in a tirade.

Coley took a step toward them. They broke, scattered. Coley replaced the billy in his hip pocket. He felt a savage satisfaction for, he thought, a job well done.

Coley stood on the corner, looked down the street where the sidewalk peddlers were hawking their wares. This was the Bay, where people bought, sold and exchanged personal effects: worn suits, stained ties and laundered socks, eyeglasses to fit any face, fountain pens, a razor, bridgework with one molar missing, a chipped glass eye, a toupee. The peddlers haggled and bargained, their voices shrill in the warm air.

The storekeeper tried to chase the peddlers from where they blocked his store entrance, but to no avail. Coley knew that, after he tired of talking, the storekeeper would telephone the precinct, demand that the street be cleared.

It was Coley's job to clear the street before the desk sergeant was disturbed.

Sighing deeply, he walked into the crowd, waved his arms. "Break it up, c'mon, break it up."

Sullen, they broke slowly, reluctantly. One peddler, about to complete the sale of a stained pair of bloomers obviously too large for the frowsy woman customer, pleaded. "One minute. I finish, I go."

After a while the street was comparatively clear. Coley walked on, glanced at his wrist watch. Five after two. One hour and fifty-five minutes to go. Near the corner the flat-chested girl who worked in a disorderly house on the top floor sat in the shade of the stoop. Seeing Coley, the blonde leaned back against the iron grill, looked him in the eye, smiled.

Though there's a promise in her eyes, he thought, right now she wants nothing. She had a tough night and it's kind of warm.

She said, "Hello. Sit down a while."

Coley said, "You're growin' up. A couple more inches around that chest and you'll look like a girl. Then I'll sit down."

She seemed neither surprised nor offended. "Maybe then I won't want you to sit down."

He laughed. "I'm a gambler. I'll wait."

He walked on and for some reason he began to think of another blonde, one who was probably a lot smarter—she didn't have to work in a two-dollar joint to make a living. This broad wasn't worth any more than the deuce she commanded—the other could sit in a night club and drink her belly full of champagne cocktails, then take a guy, any guy, upstairs and demand a couple hundred bucks. And she'd be worth every nickel, and more.

He had a peculiar feeling in his thighs, as if he were in the girl's hallway, kissing her good night, kissing her hard. On the corner, he went into the cigar store, and fumbled with the telephone book and after a while he remembered the name Cangro's.

He wrote the address of Cangro's in his little black book and went outside in time to see a prowl car go by.

Coley saluted the sergeant. To himself he said, "Sit on your fat behinds, ride around like big shots while I break my hump."

Coley ordered the pickle merchant to get his barrels off the sidewalk. "It's bad enough you stink up the street without blocking it too."

"My pickles stink?"

"Yeh. Another word out of you and I'll have the Board of Health after you. Off the sidewalk ..."

The prowl car returned, pulled up at the curb. The sergeant, a well-built man with massive hands, came out of the car.

Coley thought, What the hell does Jesus Christ want? I gave him a slam. Maybe he didn't see it.

Coley saluted again. The sergeant's hand went limply to his cap, dropped heavily at his side.

He had a lean hungry look. Like a vulture, Coley thought.

In a voice as coldly assumed as his face, the sergeant said. "Where you hang out lately, Walsh?"

"Working the beat, Sergeant, working my legs off."

The sergeant grunted. "Yeh, sure. Keep your eye open around Klutz's jewelry store. He's about due for another stick-up." He stared at Coley for a few seconds. About to say something, he closed his lips, slid into the prowl car. Coley relaxed as the car pulled away from the curb.

Ahead of him a man was hurrying, a pair of worn

shoes in his left hand, patched trousers, a soiled shirt and a pair of shorts in his right hand. The man had a three-day beard. The red-rimmed eyes stared glassily ahead.

Alongside him, trying desperately to match his pace, was a buxom woman.

I can smell her from here, Coley thought, or maybe the sewer is open around the corner.

The man saw the patrolman, slowed perceptibly. The woman, trying unsuccessfully to cover her exposed breasts, uneasily pulled the torn collar of her pink blouse closer around her neck.

Coley said, "That stuff you're carrying, where'd you get it?"

"Mine," the man said hoarsely.

"His," the woman said, vigorously scratching her tousled black hair.

Coley glanced down at the man's feet. The man's gaze followed, vague fear widening his eyes.

Coley said, "Maybe the shoes you're wearing don't belong to you. They're a different size. That shirt marked fourteen won't get around your fat neck." He took the man's arm. "Let's go back to where you got the stuff."

The woman trembled. "Please, officer." Her teeth were yellow, mottled. "It's his'n. I swear it by my mother and father."

He pushed the man. "Start walking."

The woman backed away. "I got nothin' to do with this. He took it, not me."

"You come along, just for the walk. Okay, mister, where is the guy you swiped these from? Shut your mouth. I don't want to hear from you. Just show me. You too, lady, shut up."

They crossed the gutter, the man beginning to shake. "I didn't do nothing. I won the stuff in a crap game. So help me."

Coley watched the man's eyes as they were reaching

the next corner. One more block and they'd be off his beat. He heard a tiny catch of sound escape the woman's mouth. Turning quickly, he caught her looking into a dark hallway.

"Okay, hold it." He steered the man to the hallway, the woman following. "Inside, both of you."

He found the victim near the wooden door leading to the cellar, a forty-watt bulb casting a sickening glare over the nude body.

"He made me do it." The woman began to sob. "I'm a good girl. I never done this before."

"You kill this guy?" Squatting, Coley turned the man's face up. The body reeked of cheap whiskey and stale sweat. Coley slapped the bearded man twice. The man stirred, groaned and tried to roll onto his stomach. Satisfied, Coley yanked the clothes out of the shaking man's hands, dropped them on the body.

"Get up out of there and get dressed."

The man on the floor sat up, scratched his head with both hands.

The thief said, "I was hard up. I needed a drink."

Coley looked at the woman, sobbing frantically. "You can cut that out, lady."

"You—you won't arrest me, officer. I'm a good girl …"

Coley looked away. In this neighborhood if you locked up every violator of the law, you could spend a lifetime in courtrooms. However, this was more serious. He had no doubt that the woman was the bait, luring the man into the hallway for her companion to rob. Coley knew also that the same victim, even after this experience, could be lured again into a hallway by the same woman. Unbelievable, but that's how it was in this neighborhood. One stole from the other, and in turn was robbed.

He remembered when he was a kid, the gang would go to the public swimming pool on Rivington Street. Many times somebody would come up from the pool to find his sneakers stolen. The victim would immediately go to another of the open lockers and steal a pair to replace his. The new victim, Coley knew, would do likewise. At the end of the day the last sucker with no one to steal from would go home barefooted. At the beginning of the next day, he could then visit the public baths to look for a pair of sneakers to fit him.

Coley thought, I always did wonder who was the very last guy to get stuck.

Coley cried, "All right, beat it. But don't let me catch you on this beat again, you or that floozie."

He watched them go, holding onto each other, stumbling in their eagerness to leave the scene.

His wrist watch said three-fifty. It was time to meet the four-to-midnight patrolman assigned to posts forty-one, forty-two and forty-three.

## Three

Thirty-fourth Street was crowded with people, hustling and bustling, adeptly avoiding contact with each other. The cadence of voices was a steady drone of sound, horns blared, sweaty truck drivers leaning out from behind their wheels to swear at the private cars and taxis in their path. While the drivers argued, shirtless boys pushed hand trucks loaded with garments across the gutter or around the stalled cars. A hand truck filled with parcels slammed into the rear fender of a red and white Buick, toppled. The car driver came out, hot words on his lips, and stood over the frantic boy sweeping the packages up from the gutter.

The corner candy stores were doing a flourishing business, people lined up, gulping sodas, chocolate, red and pale colored drinks in thick glasses.

"Egg cream," a man ordered, the sweat running down his face. "A man could die from thirst."

The counterman slapped a glass on the marble slab, some of the chocolate drink spilling. "I got only two hands, my friend. Give with the ten cents already."

"You didn't wash the glass."

"What can you catch? We got no sick people on Seventh Avenue. Maybe you should go up on Park Avenue."

Shapely girls, somewhat thin and gaunt, hurried up the street. Eyes cold against the men who stared openly, they walked stiffly, their hatboxes dangling from gloved wrists. A boy of eleven, standing over three piles of Jewish newspapers spread on the curb, cried, "H'ya, get y'mornin' papers *Tag, Forvetz, Freiheit.*"

A mounted policeman came down the street. His brown horse held its head high, the shiny body sleek and trim. The policeman pulled gently on the reins and the horse sidled close to the curb. The policeman motioned to the boy, who quickly gathered up his newspapers and, bow-legged with the load, staggered away.

The policeman yanked at the reins and the horse trotted away, its short tail stiff. The boy came out from where he'd sought refuge among a group of men.

His papers back on the curb, he chanted, "H'ya, get y'papers. *Forvetz, Tag, Freiheit.*"

Everybody was sweating in the Garment Center— the people in the street, the boys, the policeman, the horse—everybody except the girls with the hatboxes.

The elevator shot up to the twelfth floor with such speed Coley felt as if he'd left his stomach behind. As soon as the door slid open, he stepped out, turned in time to catch the operator's pitying smile. The door closed with a minimum of noise, then the overhead green light blinked off.

His leather heels clicked noisily on the marble floor as he went up the hallway, glancing at the names on each floor. At the end of the hall, he stopped.

CANGRO, INC.

And in the lower right hand corner of the double door,

JOSEPH CANTOR, Pres.

The circular reception room was small. A telephone operator was behind a glass partition which filled a space between two benches. In the center of the room was a glass-topped coffee table piled with periodicals and a copy of the *Times*.

Heatedly discussing the dress market, two men sat on one of the benches. The operator pulled out a plug, inserted another.

Coley spoke through the hole in the window. "Miss, is there a Mille who works here?"

"Mille? Mille Raft?"

"I'll take a chance on her if you've got no other Mille."

"Your name, please?"

"Coley Walsh."

She plugged in, spoke so softly into the mouthpiece that Coley couldn't catch a word.

Yanking out the plug, she said, "Miss Raft is tied up. I'll try again in a few minutes."

A man came in on noiseless feet. His hands were big as hams and his shoulders were so wide Coley wondered if he'd stuffed the jacket with telephone books.

After giving Coley a quick look, he said to the operator, "Tell Joseph Cantor Jimmy Luckman wants to talk to him."

Without looking around, she said, "You have an appointment with Mr. Cantor?"

"Just tell him, and I'll have one."

"Mr. Cantor is a busy man."

He growled. "So'm I, lady. Mr. Cantor won't like it if you keep me waiting. You gonna call him or do I walk right through that door marked 'No Admittance'?"

She plugged in. "Mr. Cantor. I'm sorry, Mr. Cantor, but there's a Mr. Luckman ... Mr. Cantor?"

She looked around at the man. "Mr. Cantor didn't say anything. He just hung up."

Luckman chuckled. "Maybe he had a stroke."

The 'No Admittance' door swung open and a short, squarely-built man in shirt sleeves burst into the room. The dead cigar clutched in his teeth was tilted so sharply it almost touched his big nose.

"*Momser*," the stocky man cried, shaking his fist at Luckman. "Didn't I tell you to keep away from me?"

The man wasn't perturbed. "Where can we talk, Cantor?"

The buzzer sounded but the operator had lost interest in her switchboard.

Cantor pulled the cigar out of his mouth. "To you, I don't talk." He spat dryly. "This for you."

"We could straighten out our little troubles."

He pointed to the hall door. "Trouble I eat up. Out!"

When Luckman laughed, Cantor pushed him. "Out, I said."

Luckman's smile vanished. "Don't do that again, Cantor."

"This is my place. I say out." Again he pushed Luckman, first with one hand, then with both, so hard that Luckman staggered.

Luckman clenched his fists. "One more push and I'll tear you apart."

Coley chuckled to himself. This was like a TV Mack Sennett movie. Now Luckman was supposed to punch wildly and Cantor would duck under and get kicked in his behind.

But Luckman wasn't following the script. When Cantor shoved him again, his hand disappeared into his pocket and came out clutching a knife.

"I'll cut your heart out," Luckman shouted.

The girl at the switchboard moaned, collapsed. The man sitting on the bench clasped his hands together and prayed. Cantor, his eyes on the knife, stood his ground as if paralyzed.

Luckman came after Cantor who, suddenly awakened out of his trance, backed away, crying, "Police! Murderer! Help!"

Coley hit Luckman on the back of the neck. The man went down, rolled away, and came up on his feet in one easy motion. Snarling, he turned on Coley, lunged. Sidestepping quickly, Coley grasped the man's wrist, twisted sharply. Luckman cried out in pained surprise, the knife clattering to the floor. Disdain in his manner, Coley pushed Luckman, sending the big man sprawling at the feet of the man praying and shaking on the bench.

Cantor pointed dramatically to the door. "Lousy gangster, out! Knives you use on me? Tell your lousy bosses, while I live this place will be Joseph Cantor's."

Coley picked up the knife. "You wanna make a complaint? I'll take him down to the station house."

Cantor looked startled. "Station house? Who needs that business?"

"You scared of him? He tried to stab you."

Cantor was angered at Coley's stupidity. "Me scared of my good friend?" He bent over, playfully slapped the face of the man who was now sitting on the floor. "You are not my friend? Speak up!" He slapped him harder. "Tell him you're Cantor's friend."

The man cried, "You slap me again, you sonofabitch, I'll kill you."

"See?" Cantor said triumphantly. "To a stranger he would talk like that?"

Luckman came to his feet, the blood full in his face.

"What for you buttin' in?" he said to Coley.

Coley said, "You keep talking and I won't listen to Cantor. I'll run you down the station house for making a pass at me with that knife. So while I'm in this good mood, why don't you beat it?"

Luckman blinked as Coley's words slammed into him. "I was just talkin'," he said lamely. "I'll see you, Cantor." He backed to the door. "Just a lousy five minutes, that's all I wanted." He turned, opened the door and ran out.

Cantor closed the door. Now that the man was gone, Cantor's face was a sickly yellow.

"You see that knife?" To the man sitting on the bench, "You see, Kessel? He coulda killed me dead." He turned to Coley. "You all right, boy?"

"If I wasn't, I'd've never let him walk out on both legs."

"Like a herring he could have cut you up."

"He could've cut you too."

"Me, I'm so old, I don't even bleed. My life I've lived already."

"You're okay, Pop."

"You, boy, you're okay. I like you. Maybe I buy you a drink or something, detective?"

"How'd you know I was a cop?"

Cantor chuckled. "I just know. Or maybe I think you are too nice to carry that big gun unless you are a cop. A name you got?"

"Coley Walsh."

"Mm-m." Cantor played with his chin. "You come maybe to buy a dress wholesale? We don't sell retail trade but you I can afford to give a dress, a present for your wife ... or sweetheart."

Coley said, "I came to see somebody called Mille and they're giving me a hard time."

"Mille? Mille don't tell me she got a policeman friend."

Coley shrugged. "She doesn't know she's got one."

Cantor said to the operator. "You all right? That louse, he could have killed me." He touched Coley's arm. "I send her out. Coley, next time you come, remember I owe you a dress."

Coley watched him go through the swinging door with the oval glass, then, curious, Coley looked through the glass to see what was on the other side. Girls scurried over the carpeted floor, some clutching papers in their fists; others, obviously models, faces painted into stiff masks, pranced about before the full length mirrors on the wall.

In a few moments he saw her come down the hall and stop before a tri-jointed mirror. Moving into various positions, she studied the blue woolen dress she wore. Coley waited until the operator got busy on a telephone call, then, pushing open the swinging door, went through. Girls and men brushed by him, but nobody questioned his presence.

He caught her eye in the mirror, held them. "Very pretty," he said, touching the soft cloth of the dress. "A dozen would set me back a month's pay."

Her eyes weren't blue as he'd thought. They were a grayish-green.

She said, "You wouldn't look good in this type dress. You're not one of the buyers?"

"Everybody's a potential buyer."

Recognition came suddenly. "You!"

He smiled. "I could be wrong, but that tip you dropped in that cab, you know, that Cangro stuff, gave me the idea it was done deliberately."

"You could be very wrong." There was no warmth in her smile as she tried to brush him off. "I've got work to do, so if you'll excuse me ..."

Coley said, "You and me got a lunch date."

She said coldly, "I'm not that hungry."

Joseph Cantor came into view from around the bend. "Mille? All day I got to wait? Oh, it's you, Coley. Mille, my friend Coley Walsh wants to talk with you."

Coley said, "Mille won't talk to strangers."

"What strangers? Mille, this is my friend. You didn't hear me? Coley, I thanked you ...?"

"Mille has lunch with me, we're even."

Cantor was surprised. "Mille, my friend wants to buy you lunch, he's got trouble?"

Mille said, banteringly, "That an order, Mr. Cantor?"

"A favor, my little girl. For me. I owe this boy my life, so lunch you can't have with him?"

Mille sighed. "How can I refuse the boss?"

Cantor said, "Coley, you come again?"

Coley could feel this was not a routine question. Cantor wanted Coley to visit him.

Coley said, "That's up to Mille."

Cantor pointed his finger at her. "Mille, I like to see Coley again ..."

They found seats in a Howard Johnson restaurant and ordered roast beef sandwiches and coffee. Waiting for the order Coley watched Mille sip cold water from the frosted tumbler, her big serious eyes moving restlessly around the room.

Coley said softly, "You look like you want to be saved."

She leaned forward, her eyes on his lips. "I don't understand."

Resentment slurred his words. "Having lunch with a cop isn't exactly your idea of having a good time."

She frowned. "I didn't know you were a cop. Anyway, I'm here."

"On your boy friend's orders."

"If I didn't want to go to lunch with you, Mr. Cantor nor anybody else could have forced me. And, for your information, Mr. Cantor is not my boy friend."

For some reason, he enjoyed her discomfiture. "If I

got the wrong impression, I'm sorry. He kept calling you his Mille, like you belonged to him."

She became angry. "And if I did? Every model is part of her employer's harem. Isn't that what you've heard?"

His gaze moved slowly over her beautiful face. "I don't believe it. I don't care. From now on you're gonna be the big thing in my life."

Her mood changed. "You're being silly. You don't know me. You saw me once—"

"One minute, one hour; I can't measure time by the clock. From the first second I saw you in that cab, you had me dreaming crazy things."

The waitress brought the sandwiches and coffee, and left. Coley offered Mille the catsup bottle.

She shook her head. "One hundred and eighteen pounds is all I can afford to carry so no catsup, and you can have my potatoes."

Coley laughed. "One-eighty for me, and I can afford another five pounds." After dousing his potatoes with big red blobs, he cut a square of beef and bread, lifted them on his fork, watched the gravy drip for a second, then pushed them into his mouth.

She smiled. "You look hungry."

The muscles stood out in ridges along his jaw line as he chewed. "Where were you going the other night in the cab?"

"Home to my apartment in Brooklyn. President Street."

"I thought all models lived around Times Square, in hotels or in swanky flats."

The anger returned. "You must have read a lot of dirty books in your day."

Coley touched her hand. "I didn't mean to work you up like that. Honest, I was only trying to kid you, but I guess I don't know how. What does a guy like me say to a beautiful girl he likes more than anybody he's ever met in his life? So he tries to make an impression, be funny. Only I'm not the comedian type. Don't be sore at me."

She shrugged. "I'm not sore, not really."

"This Cantor, he seems like a nice guy."

Simply she said, "He's the sweetest person in the world, second only to Mrs. Cantor. I got the job with Cangro through the agency, my first real steady job. Oh, I had other jobs, waitress, counter girl in Woolworth's, even modeling for Benrus watches and Gold hosiery. Those jobs didn't last. The first week at Cangro, Mr. Cantor invited me to his house for a Friday night dinner. He must have seen how lonesome I was for folks, and hungry for decent home cooked meals. Everybody working for Cangro has at one time or another gone to the Cantors for a *Shabbas* dinner." She hesitated, but he looked so interested, she continued her story. "Mrs. Cantor liked me, I liked her. She reminded me so much of my mother. We talked of my home in Pitston. I cried a little and Mrs. Cantor cried too."

"You had a crying good time."

She smiled. "Guess we did. Anyway, Mrs. Cantor said no girl should live alone in a big city like New York. A girl should live with someone, in case she got sick or something. The Cantors had a son who was killed in Korea. No other children. I didn't know it but Mrs. Cantor was more lonesome than I was. So I moved into the upstairs apartment in their private house. I've been very happy living with very nice people."

Coley finished his coffee. "Who was that character in the cab that night?"

"Michael Winters? Michael is a buyer from Chicago. Every time he comes to New York he likes me to show him the town."

"Tonight you could do the same for me."

She began to pull on her gloves. "I should get back to the office."

"I'll pick you up around eight."

"I've got a job."

"Another buyer?"

"It's part of my job."

"I gotta become a buyer of Cangro's dresses to get a date?"

She found that amusing. "No, Coley. Some other time perhaps ..."

"Tomorrow? The day after? After that I go back to the four o'clock shift."

"Some day next week."

"I'll see you a week from Friday night. It's my day off."

She got up from the table. "All right, Coley. Around eight ..."

## Four

Dressed in his new gray flannel suit, Coley took the Lexington Avenue express and got off on Utica Avenue in Brooklyn. Walking up the subway steps to the street, he mopped his face. It had been hot and sticky riding in the subway. In the street the temperature was ten degrees cooler.

Before entering the florist shop on the corner, Coley took inventory of his cash assets. He had twenty-eight dollars and thirty cents, and it was ten days to pay day. The rent was paid, the installment on his uniform wasn't due for another month and Mom had a couple of dollars.

Twenty-eight dollars should cover the cost of a dinner and a cab trip from Brooklyn to New York and back again. That didn't leave much for the movie he wanted to see at Radio City. He figured out that eight bucks for the cab, both ways, and three-sixty for the movies left over sixteen dollars for dinner ... Now, if he didn't eat like a pig ...

He went into the shop and bought a wrist corsage

of yellow roses.

The Cantors lived in a two-story brick and veneer corner house. Even rows of bushes bordered the white stone walk, and a massive green lawn sloped gently from the house to the two-car garage. Water gushed out of a bronze maiden's mouth into a small circular pool set in the center of the lawn. A pair of four-cornered nozzle sprays revolved slowly, sprinkling the grass to a glistening sheen in the sun's fading rays. A small puddle of water had formed on the stone walk leading to the side of the house. The puddle had grown a drop at a time, and when Coley turned into the alley, he was forced to hop over the water.

The door at the side of the house, Mille had told him, opened to a narrow wooden stairway that led to the Cantor's apartment on the first level and to Mille's apartment one flight up. As Coley reached out to open the street door, it was pushed open by a tall, heavy-set man, gray temples giving him a distinguished look. Coley stepped back, suspicion gnawing in his mind.

"Oh, Coley." Mille came into view. "I'm terribly sorry."

She looked sweet in the low cut white dress, her hair curling in gold ringlets behind her ears. And so flustered.

Angry, Coley said, "Looks like I'm getting a stand-up."

She touched his arm in an impulsive gesture. "I just completely forgot until this morning when I remembered I had a date with Peter. Oh, excuse me; Coley Walsh, Peter Carlyle. I went crazy trying to look you up in the telephone book. You weren't listed. I even tried to get you through police headquarters. It was stupid of me. Forgive me, Coley, please?"

The self-reproach in her eyes melted away his anger. "I'd rather not forgive you. I'd rather sweep you into that cab. But I guess I have no choice."

Amusement danced across the other man's face.

"I'd like to add my apologies too." He had a firm voice, young and full of power.

"You," Coley said, "I don't forgive."

Carlyle laughed. "You are taking this graciously."

"I don't feel gracious, believe me. I'd like to kick down a wall."

"I'd feel the same way."

Mille said, helplessly, "If you're not still angry, next Friday, Coley?"

Carlyle still found the situation funny. "You're forgetting, Mille. We have a date for a sail."

"I thought it was for two weeks from now. Give me a ring, Coley."

Coley swallowed the hot words that came up sour and vile from inside him. All of a sudden he felt small and unimportant and he didn't like it. But, he thought, blowing my top isn't going to help things. He didn't want to hurt her. The regret she'd expressed in her words and manner had been ample apology.

"Okay," Coley said, "I'll call you in a day or so."

Carlyle's handshake was hearty. "See you again, Coley."

When they'd gone, Coley walked slowly out to the street. Remembering, he held up the corsage box, in a sudden burst of temper flung it out into the gutter, and when a car crushed the box under its wheels he felt a dull satisfaction.

From behind him Joseph Cantor said, "Right now you want an explosion should blow up the whole world."

Coley spoke over his shoulder, "This Carlyle one of your damn buyers?"

Cantor shrugged. "What buyer? Carlyle is a big businessman. Stocks, bonds, a towel-supply outfit, a moneylending company. A millionaire. I meet him once when he comes up to my office; he's got money to invest, maybe I want to take in for a partner? I tell him partners Joe Cantor don't need. So he shakes hands with me, like a gentleman, and goes his way."

"He shook hands with Mille, too."

Cantor looked hurt. "I shouldn't introduce such a gentleman to my Mille? Come inside the house. My missus wants to meet the man who saved her husband's life."

Coley sighed. "If you'll promise to get me stinking drunk."

Cantor laughed, taking Coley's arm to steer him into the house.

Mrs. Cantor, tall and gray, looked out at Coley from gentle brown eyes. Her accent was faint, pleasing to the ear.

"I'm sorry about Mille, very sorry."

Coley laughed shortly. "Everybody's sorry for me. Pop, how about those drinks?"

Cantor touched a knob of what looked like a television set. The door swung open and shiny bottles and glasses came into view. Without asking, Cantor poured yellow liquid into short glasses.

"Slivovitz," he said. "You don't like, I give you Scotch."

"Poison," Mrs. Cantor said, "is poison, slivovitz or Scotch."

Coley took the glass out of Cantor's hand. "To Mille," he said, "and to you, Mom." He drank the liquor in one swift gulp, gasped. "Holy! My tongue is on fire. Now my stomach."

Joseph Cantor refilled Coley's glass. "A baby," he said, "they give slivovitz. When my mother, she should rest in peace, got tired feeding me the breast, she gave me slivovitz with a nipple."

Coley sat down on a club chair, stretched his legs. "Pop, Carlyle must be loaded."

Cantor clucked. "He takes my Mile to the best places in New York. A real gentleman."

"You said that before, and I'm getting self-conscious."

Cantor laughed. "You, Coley, you're a gentleman with a cap; he is a gentleman with a high hat."

Coley got up and walked to the screen door. The puddle had grown, or so it seemed. The sprayer rotated noiselessly on its swivel. A bee skirted the hedges, abruptly shied away from the fine spray hanging like a mist over the grass. The sun had faded and swift dusk was falling over the city.

Coley turned. "How do you compete against a guy like Carlyle? Dinner at the Ritz, box seats to a show, coffee at the Copa. That's the kind of a life girls lap up. A poor slob doesn't stand a chance."

Mrs. Cantor straightened the candelabra. "Some girls, if they like a boy, they eat in the Automat."

Coley shook his head. "A two-bit movie or a Broadway show makes all the difference in the world."

Cantor ran his forefinger around the rim of the glass. "Money is all right, but health is more important."

Coley stood over him. "What if you haven't got either?"

They stared at him in disbelief. Mrs. Cantor said, "You look strong …"

"Sure," Coley said, "I'm so damned strong, with one hand I can lift my crippled son up to the ceiling."

It was quiet for a moment. Cantor murmured, "I didn't know."

Coley said, "I shouldn't be shooting off my mouth like that."

Mrs. Cantor excused herself. "Candles I must light. It's *Shabbas*."

"Candles," Joseph Cantor laughed. "Such a waste. It wouldn't be better if you send the money the candles cost to charity?"

"It's *Shabbas*," she said quietly. "I light candles for you, for me."

"For me you don't light nothing. The devil wants to find me, with light you don't have to supply him."

Coley watched as she placed a white shawl around her shoulders. After lighting two candles in the silver candlesticks standing on the buffet, she blew out the match, dropped it onto the ashtray.

She drew the shawl over her head as she said, "For you, my husband, for me, it don't hurt."

She turned her face to the candles and began to pray, her body swaying. The Hebrew words were clear, vibrant.

"Blessed art Thou, O Lord our God, King of the universe, who hast sanctified us by Thy commandments and commanded us to kindle the Sabbath-light."

Coley listened and he felt a peculiar ache inside him, a reverence he'd never felt before. Mrs. Cantor looked taller, more stately, the light giving her face a warmth and glow that made her seem beautiful. Coley's glance skipped to Cantor, standing near the table, the empty whiskey glass still clutched in his hand. The man's face had lost all trace of expression, then as Coley watched, a vein throbbed in Cantor's forehead, like a blue violin string being plucked. Cantor's thick lips which had been twisted in scorn softened, and now there was complete respect and a touch of fear in his manner.

Mrs. Cantor's voice shook with emotion. "Enlighten our eyes so that this light shall never be extinguished. Let Thy countenance shine upon us and grant us salvation. Amen."

Joseph Cantor's lips formed "a-men" as he turned away. "You feel better, Bessie?"

She dropped the shawl onto her shoulders. "When I die, Yussel, you live like you want. While I live this will be a Jewish house."

He gave her a strained, sardonic laugh. "I never tell you what you should do in this house. It is yours. I only suggest what is not right. Suggest."

"To get a girl to help you in the kitchen, to clean,

two girls, three, that is wrong?"

"When I am a cripple, I get a dozen maids."

He chortled. "To clean like you want, you need a dozen. The candles I suggest—"

"When I die to your second wife you suggest."

He pulled at his lower lip. "In fifty years.

She laughed. "I wait."

He placed his palms against her cheek and drew her head to him and kissed her gently "A kiss on *Shabbas* never hurt nobody."

Coley stared. The man was crazy. First he argued, then he kissed her. First she was one of his office help, then his sweetheart. First he yelled as if he had no respect for his wife, then he spoke to her and held her as if they were sweet sixteen and very much in love. You couldn't figure a screwball like that.

Coley said, "So long, I'm getting out of here. Thanks ..."

Cantor cried, "Where you running like a crazy man? You just got here"

Coley waved his hand. "I got a date to rob a bank. 'Bye."

## Five

Coley stood on the pier stringpiece and looked down into the black dimpled river, a sheet of crinkled cellophane in the moonlight. A brief wind rippled against the low tide. In a few minutes, the river would begin its run for high tide. The water moved sluggishly, as if reluctant to change direction.

Coley ran his hands over his nude body, wiped away a piece of green moss. His toes gripping the edge of the stringpiece, he stretched his arms up, as high as he could reach, swung them quickly back and dived. In mid-air, he touched his toes, his shimmering body knifing the water so cleanly only a small splash fountained up.

The water was cool, invigorating. In another week it would be October, and too cold for swimming in the East River. Then, if he wanted a swim he could use the public baths pool on Allen Street. Somehow he liked the river better.

Maybe it's too clean in the baths, he thought. A bum like me gets used to dirt, likes it, eats it. All my life I've been swimming in dirt. But it's gonna be different soon. It's got to be.

He floated on his back for a while, looked up at the cloudless sky, counted the stars. The new moon hung like an orange ball over a Brooklyn pier. Idly, he wondered what would happen if the moon suddenly dropped into the river. Boy, what a splash!

He stared at the moon and suddenly it was gone and Mille's warm face filled his eyes. Thinking of her, he felt sudden resentment. Four times he'd taken her out, twice to the movies, once to a Broadway musical, the last time to Central Park. She hadn't said anything, yet he could tell by her manner this wasn't what she wanted. This was too tame, too cheap. Peter Carlyle did a lot better by her.

Last night he'd held her body tight against him. She'd looked up at him, a funny look in her eyes. What the hell you want for your couple bucks, they seemed to be asking. She'd said nothing. Even when he'd said good night, she hadn't answered him. The door had closed softly after her yet to him it sounded as loud as if she'd slammed it in his face. Go home, you bum!

He tried to reason: then how come she still goes out with you? And he could find no reasonable answer.

Coley felt something soft against his head. He turned quickly, slapped away the garbage. He ducked his head, came up blowing salty water in a spray. Slowly he swam in a smooth breast stroke toward the side of the pier that touched cobblestoned South Street. Inches from the pier, he swam in darkness which to him was warm and comforting. Here in the nude he felt free. Here he was alone. Here he could think.

Between the pier and the street bulkhead was a triangular piece of dry beach. Stopping to rest, his feet squished in the soft mud. He yanked at a wire tangled around his knee, heard the squeaking, the tiny feet scurrying over gravel. Then in the moonlight he saw the white-bellied water rats gnawing on the shapeless lump on the beach. He threw the wire in an arc. The squeaking stopped. The rats had disappeared noiselessly.

Coley swam back to the center of the pier, to the wooden ladder nailed to the pilings. As he pulled himself out of the water, he heard the car moving onto the pier. Careful not to slip on the broken slat in the center of the ladder, he crept up until he could peer over the stringpiece. The car rolled to a stop barely ten feet from him. It was a radio car, the white-lettered POLICE staring out in bold relief on the green background.

Coley breathed a sigh of relief. If the people in the car had been a man and woman, it would have been a heck of a job to get to his clothes stacked on the newspaper at the end of the pier.

Coley pulled himself onto the stringpiece. "Hi," he called out.

The car door opened and a blue-coated figure, holding a cigarette cupped in his right hand, stepped out. Smoke ran out of his nose in gray curls.

"What the hell?" the patrolman said.

A second patrolman came out of the car. "One of them exhibitionists," he said. "Never can tell where you'll find them. Hey, that you, Walsh? For Chris' sakes, you trying to get pinched? I'd like to hood an eleven-forty on you."

Coley laughed. "Eleven-forty hell, my fly ain't open. You guys got soft jobs, sitting on your big behinds, riding around like the Mayor, while guys like me get fallen arches."

"What for you go swimming in this crap? You a psycho?"

Coley bent over the bundle of clothing; found his shorts and undershirt. "I like it," he said. "Try it some time. See how the blackness soothes your nerves, gives you a chance to think."

The patrolmen exchanged looks. "You gotta wear trunks; you know that."

Coley stepped into his trousers, one foot at a time, tucked in the bottom of his white short-sleeved sport shirt. "You like 'em, you wear them. So long, fellers, see you around."

"Walsh, how come you ain't packing your .38? You lose it maybe?"

Coley touched his hip where regulation demanded he wear his service revolver at all times.

"Yeh," he said, "I lost it in a drawer up in my house."

"You'll get in a jam one of these days."

"So long ..."

"Don't forget trunks next time you go swimming. You're a big boy now. Showing off won't get you nothing but a date with the Bellevue psycho doctor."

Coley hurried home to shave and dress. Tonight he had a date with Pat Gund, political leader of the assembly district. On Gund, Coley was convinced, hinged his entire future in the Police Department. And if Gund helped him get a transfer to a division, Coley's dream would come true. There'd be money, lots of money for Billy, for Mom, and enough to make Mille's smile brighten.

Eyes closed tightly against the spray, Mile stood under the shower, turned to needlepoint fineness, the warm water moving around her like a winding sheet, swathing her body in clinging wetness. She reached out, turned off the shower, stood there for a minute, the water running clown the white bathing cap, down her face and body. She opened her eyes, blinked to ease the smartness caused by the soap which had managed to find its way past the lids.

Pushing open the glass stall door, she stepped out onto the green rubber mat before the full-length mirror, yanked a heavy Turkish towel out of the door rack, dried herself slowly. She pulled off the cap, let it drop on the tile floor, shook her head until the blonde hair opened loosely around her shoulders. Wiping her ample breasts, first one then the other, she smiled grimly at the gold coat of tan that ran from her head to the nipples and from the thighs to the toes. Between, was a big patch of skin, startlingly white.

Mr. Cantor hadn't liked the tan. In fact, he'd been quite incensed.

He'd cried, "Now it looks good. What happens when you wear evening gowns? You model clothes or do you advertise Madame Furtz's health camp?"

She'd promised, come next summer, she'd stay out of the sun, the same promise she'd made the year before. In her heart she knew that next summer or the summers after that she would not, could not, resist basking in the warm sun with as little clothes on as possible.

She ran the towel down a thigh, lifted her foot onto the sink, the easier to reach it. Then the other leg received the same treatment. Dry, she stood before the mirror, her gaze moving slowly over her body, her forehead creasing in a frown.

She squeezed the flesh over each hip. Was she gaining weight? It couldn't be. These days she was eating hardly anything. But, she knew despite medical testimony to the contrary, in her special case whatever she ate turned immediately to fat. To put on weight was easy. To lose weight was a full-scale operation involving sweat and starvation.

She pulled the bathroom scales out from under the sink, regulated the pointer to the zero marker. She held her breath as she stepped up. The numbered wheel turned swiftly. She said a silent prayer, "one eighteen ... one eighteen."

The indicator showed one hundred and twenty pounds. Chagrin showed in her face. Then suddenly she remembered the towel around her shoulders. She flung it from her. The indicator showed the towel had weighed six ounces.

Mille thought, that was losing weight the easy way. Now if I'd used a bath towel ...

She laughed, returned the scales to its accustomed place in the far corner under the sink.

The dusting powder came out of the medicine chest, and with the aid of the giant puff, she powdered herself liberally with the violet-scented talcum.

Mille picked up the blue and white polka-dot robe from where it lay on the clothes hamper, shook it open, slipped into it. Before she'd go to bed she'd don a nightgown.

Somehow, she could never sleep in the nude. Once on a hot summer's night, she had taken off her nightgown, then stayed awake half the night reassuring herself that the blanket was up around her middle. She preferred nightgowns. Pajamas were a nuisance, the legs rolling up, annoying.

Mille found a pack of cigarettes in the living room. She lit one and, humming a tune, moved noiselessly across the cotton rug to the secretary. She found her fountain pen, a memento of her high school days, writing paper, an envelope and a stamp. After taking a ten-dollar bill from her wallet, she zippered it closed. Abruptly changing her mind, she opened the zipper again and slipped out another five dollars.

Sorry, Mom, I'm kind of broke this week. Clothes. You understand, Mom. Next week I'll send you twenty-five.

Comfortably seated in a high backed chair, she dated the paper and wrote, Dear Mom—

She leaned back in her chair, her body slumping, bare legs spread wide under the table. What could she write this time?

The weather's fine. Working hard and in the best of health. That was in every letter. So what's new? Coley Walsh, he's new. She felt that surge of excitement that ran up her leg to her navel; a funny kind of electric tremor, every time she saw him, thought of him.

Coley Walsh, a dark-haired crazy kind of guy with a fresh mouth and big lips that always curled in a half sneer. Honest to God, Mom, I don't love him. I like him a little ... there's something about him that intrigues me, but that's not love.

I'm still dating Peter Carlyle. Is forty too old, Mom? I don't think so. Peter is the most fascinating man I've ever met. Peter is rich but you wouldn't want your little Mille to hold that against a wonderful guy? Peter is such a serious man at times, as if all the world's troubles have been dumped on his back. Mom, I've got a sneaking suspicion that one of these days Mr. Peter Carlyle will ask me to become Mrs. Peter Carlyle. Oh, well, something to dream about ...

She sighed, leaned over the writing paper. She put a colon after "Dear Mom." What to write? She caught her lips in her teeth, biting them.

After pondering a few more minutes, she wrote:

I'm well. Hope everything is all right in Pitston. Does that nurse still come in to give your leg a weekly massage? Remember what the doctor said. Every treatment will get your leg muscles to function that much faster. So don't let me hear again that you discontinued those massages. Lots of people have strokes. Many of these people have been made good as new through these massages. Next week, I'll try to send you some extra money. Give my love to Uncle Si. Tell him not to work too hard. (As if I have to tell him that.) You should see the price of bread in the city.

Twenty cents a pound! And they blame it on the poor farmer. They should know what you get for a bushel of wheat.

I'm tired, Mom, so I'll close with love and kisses.
Mille.

P.S. Mom, please put some flowers on Dad's grave for me. I'll try hard to make it home for Christmas.
Mille.

After she had addressed, sealed and stamped the envelope, she sat on the couch and read a detective story magazine. When the blood and thunder began to pall, she threw the magazine aside, stretched out full length on the couch, hands under her head, staring up at the ceiling.

The sound of the buzzer startled her. She glanced at the clock on the mantlepiece over the fireplace. After midnight. She frowned, looked down at her naked thighs, closed the robe. The sound of the buzzer seemed to jump at her.

"Who is it?" She swung her feet to the floor, stood up. The voice was muffled. "Why don't you open the door and find out?"

She unlocked the door, opened it. Coley looked so tired, his forehead smudged with soot. She could smell the liquor from six feet away. "What is it, Coley?"

"Gimme a drink like a good kid."

She hesitated, went into the kitchen. When she came back into the living room a few minutes later, Coley was stretched out on the couch, his head resting on the chair arm, his jacket a heaping pile on the floor. He swung around, took the glass from her hand.

Coley said, "I don't like drinking alone."

She picked up his jacket, laid it across the club chair. "You look as if you've done all right up to now."

Coley grinned. "A couple drinks ... Damn that Pat Gund. Who the hell does he think he's crapping?"

She watched him gulp his drink. "Somebody I

know?"

"A toilet-paper politician. Aw, the hell with him. I'll do all right without him. Mille, I'm gonna get you so much money I'll build a golden fence around you, and you'll be mine, no more Cangro, no more buyers, nobody but me."

She said wearily, "Coley, you're drunk."

He got up on his elbow, looked her over slowly. "You look good," he said softly.

Suddenly aware of her nakedness under the robe, she felt the warm flush come up from her throat and spread over her face. She saw the amused twist of his lips and looked away, angry with herself.

Coley smiled. "I said a dirty word? We're not kids, Mille. The more I see you, the more I want you. I can't tell you in pretty poetry how I feel. All I know is I want to kiss you so hard I'd melt right into you. I'm talking about love, honey, real honest-to-God love."

"What you're talking about isn't love."

He shrugged, lay back on the couch. "Maybe you're right. Get me another drink, baby, like a good girl."

"If I were a good girl, I'd send you home."

"One lousy drink, and I get a speech." The clock on the mantlepiece chimed the half-hour. He lay his arm over his face. "Take it easy on the soda this time."

Sighing in defeat, Mille went into the kitchen and mixed him another drink. The glass was too full to be carried safely, so she sipped off some of the liquid as she returned to the living room.

He lifted his head, drank half the glass in one gulp, lay back on the couch. "Damn that Gund. Just a lousy favor. He turned me down."

"Perhaps he couldn't do it."

"If I'd got the dough on the line, he'd do it."

"He could be honest."

He finished the drink, rolled the glass on the floor. "Mille, I think I'm sick."

"Can I get you something?"

"Thousand dollar bills, a truck load."

"You're not sick, you're hungry."

"What would you do for me if I had a hundred grand?"

"Go home, Coley."

"What the hell's so special at home? Give me a kiss, baby."

"Coley, please. It's going on one o'clock."

"I ask for one kiss and I get arguments. Kiss me."

She looked down at him. Stretched out on the couch, he looked so tall ... and strong. Kiss him, Mille, and he'll go home. Kiss him because you want him to go.

"All right," she said. "If that's the only way to get rid of you."

She bent over him, her lips brushing his in a peck. Before she could straighten up, he'd grabbed a fistful of hair, holding her lips against him. First there was the taste of Scotch, sweet and thick and a little nauseating, then it was Coley, delicious, stupefying.

One kiss, Mille, so he can go home.

Suddenly his hand was inside her robe, against her thigh. A feeling of revulsion swept over her.

"No, Coley." The words were tight in her throat.

She tried to pull away but he held onto her wrist, while his other hand was alive, pulling at her robe. Consternation and anger in her face, she struck at him with her free hand. Stunned, he released her. She didn't stop, moving in, punching with her tiny fists.

He blocked the left but the right landed on his eye. "Hey," he shouted, "you'll mark me up."

She stood there gasping. "Next time," she said, "I'll give it to you where it really hurts."

He began to laugh. "You are the craziest broad I ever met."

Icy gray eyes drilled through him. "Now get out, before I really prove that."

He said, "What did I do that was so terrible? A guy wants to love a girl so bad his throat gets tight with the smell of her, his stomach tightens into a knot every time he thinks of her body against his. Is that wrong? I wanted a kiss. That's all I wanted. Then your lips touched mine and all of a sudden my body was on fire. For that you give me a shiner?"

Her lips quivered. She tried to control herself but found the situation suddenly humorous. She burst out laughing, Coley joining.

"Okay," she said, drying her eyes. "Now you go home."

"Yes, teacher. Monday is my day off."

"Call me ..."

## Six

It was noisy in the locker room. Locker doors creaked open, slammed shut. Voices rose and fell in a disordered cadence. Somebody laughed heartily, inadvertently kicked over a metal stool. The men were getting ready for the midnight-to-eight tour.

Coley zippered up his wool sweater, shrugged into the blue worsted coat.

He said, "Kind of cold today."

A man, lacing his high-top shoes while he sat on a metal stool, lifted his head. "You should have the Coney Island beat, then you'll see what's cold."

"No, thanks," Coley said. "I did a week around the Fulton Fish Market. Between the smell and the East River whipping cold sprays over my head, I had enough."

Coley went into the back room, glanced casually at the papers thumb-tacked onto the wooden board. There were two 'wanted' alarms, a bank-robber and a murderer; a girl of sixteen had left home two days before, never arriving at her destination, Seward Park High School; an old man had taken a walk from the

Old Men's Home on Jefferson Street, his description followed; a Chevrolet sedan had been stolen, the owner a Chinese living on Henry Street, the license number K452.

At eleven-forty-five Coley followed the men outside, where they formed ranks on the sidewalk. It was beginning to rain. People stopped to watch, amusement in their eyes. Sergeant Flynn stood stiffly, his paunch prominent. "Take your posts."

As it grew colder, the rain turned to snow, a white broken veil that covered the city with a two-inch blanket. The white snow turned gray, then muddy black. Traffic slowed and in the busier intersections, vehicles became so deadlocked Coley had to go into the slushy gutter to act as traffic cop until the snarl was untangled.

Ice formed and walking became deliberate. People hid their faces behind their coat lapels. A woman slipped, came down hard. A man helped her half-way up before her weight and his insecure footing pulled him off his feet.

Coley Walsh walked through the slush, water running down his heavy black raincoat. He stepped into a hallway, and behind the protection of the street door, shook the rain from his rubber helmeted cap. He lighted a cigarette, held it cupped in his hand, took a deep drag, blew smoke out of quivering nostrils.

He dropped the cigarette on the hall floor, stepped on it. After buttoning his coat collar and slipping the helmet over his head, he went outside to the police box affixed to the church brick building.

"Patrolman Walsh."

The sergeant sounded as if he had a bad cold. "Good to hear from you, Walsh. A cop could drown out in this rain."

"You keep talking and in a minute I probably will."

"Keep your eyes peeled for a six-year-old colored girl—"

"Huh?"

"She walked out of her Suffolk Street house an hour ago. She's kind of light, curly black hair, a small scar over the left eye. She wore a blue cotton dress and a blue and white striped sweater. Somebody may have taken her in for shelter."

"I hope so. This is no night for kids, dogs or cops."

"You'll live."

Coley walked east. One hour to go, sixty lousy minutes. It was time he checked the stores but he thought of wading through the slush, yanking at doors, crossing the rivers of rain at each corner, walking, sliding, swimming almost, and decided no sane person would try to burglarize a store in this weather.

And, he muttered aloud, crazy people belong in a nut house not in a prison ...

He stepped into a hallway, lighted a cigarette. Two cars drove up, sending a shower of black rain and snow onto the sidewalk, and parked two feet from the curb. Three men got out of the first car. The street-light caught their faces in its soft light as they hurried quickly up a flight of stairs two doors down the street. Coley recognized Patrolmen Block, Perry and Dawson, plainclothes division men. Four uniformed patrolmen came out of the second car, followed the plainclothes men up the stairs. Coley stepped out on the sidewalk, looked up at the building into which the men had vanished.

It's about time they cracked down on that gang, he thought.

Following the rules, Coley had reported the suspected place. He'd watched men going upstairs one and two at a time. At first, he'd thought they were visiting a new disorderly house. But the men had stayed for hours. The patrolman on the twelve-to-eight tour had informed Coley that the men had left the premises in the early hours of the morning. Either there'd been a stag party—which could mean the division men had an obscene movie case to handle—or the men had engaged in some form of gambling.

The next night the action had moved from the 240 building to the tenement house on the corner. The third night the men had entered the 219 apartment house.

Each time Coley had made his report. Nothing had happened, the action continuing in its new location every night. But, tonight, even before Coley could report that the 145 building was under suspicion, the division men had struck. Obviously, the inspector had had men working on the case these past few nights.

The shot sounded loud in the stillness on the night. Alerted at once, Coley flung away his butt, slipped his hand inside the raincoat as he stepped out into the rain. It was quiet. Nothing moved, nothing alive. The rain was being whipped up by the wind, slapping into his face at an angle. About to step back into the hallway to wipe the blurred vision out of his eyes, Coley tensed. A dark figure clutching a black bag, was coming down the stairs of the 145 building. It was a man, heavy in the shoulders, the trench coat collar pulled high around his ears. Suddenly his foot shot out and, a cry escaping his lips, he sprawled on the sidewalk.

Coley moved quickly, his hand tight around his revolver handle. The man came up on hands and knees. He looked up. Their eyes met and locked.

Coley said, "What's the matter, feller?"

The man straightened, swung his right arm. The bag caught Coley on the side of the head, sent him reeling. Crying out something obscene, the man picked up the bag and ran up the street, Coley after him. Twice the man slipped and almost went down. Each time he saved himself.

"Stop," Coley cried, "or I'll shoot."

He wondered at his warning. First he should shoot, then, after he brought his man down, he could shoot a bullet up in the air. Later, he could say how he had fired a warning shot, but the fugitive hadn't stopped.

The man turned into an alley. Coley raised his gun. He heard a cry behind him. He recognized one of the division men by his awkward build as being Perry. The other man could be Block or Dawson. Coley hurried after the man with the black bag, hopped over a low fence, tore his coat on a nail. The man was vaulting a three-foot railing. Coley lifted his gun, decided against it. This was a tenement district, each building jammed with people. If his bullet missed the target, somebody could get hurt.

He thought, anyway, why waste a bullet on a lousy bookie? If I can't catch that tub of lard, I should quit. He shoved the gun back in the holster, held his night stick tightly.

The man was disappearing down a cellar. Coley took two long steps, flung himself over the railing. He landed on top of the man's head, heard the grunt as the man collapsed under him, rolled hard against the wall. The air knocked out of him, Coley lay there for a long second, then he fumbled for his club, found it. The man moved. Coley brought the club down on the man's backside. The man cried out.

Coley said, "I should've laid it across your head."

He picked up the black bag, opened it, stuck his hand inside. The wetness couldn't desensitize his fingers.

Money, he thought, more money than I ever saw in my life. He could feel his pulse pounding when he thought of what he could do with it.

At, let's say, a hundred bucks a week, how long could Billy get the proper care and therapy treatment at a good hospital ... If I had the dough?

"Okay, we'll take that."

As the two division men came down the stairs, Officer Perry slipped on the last step, went down on one knee. The man on the ground stirred, rolled over.

Cursing violently, Perry kicked him viciously in the ribs. The man gasped, lay there moaning.

"Cut it out," Dawson said, "you wanna kill him?"

"So I'll kill him," Perry snarled. He turned on Coley, took the bag. "What were you looking for in that bag, buster?"

Coley said, "A cue stick. Don't take it out on me. I'm the guy who caught him, you know."

Perry's bony yellow face twitched. "I'll get you a medal."

"Don't get me anything, just keep your mouth closed."

Dawson's shoulders rolled, like a prizefighter loosening his muscles. "Cut it out, Manny. Why don't we get out of this damn rain?" He pushed on the cellar door, swung it open, yanked at the cord dangling from the ceiling. Pale yellow light formed a circle on the dusty cellar door. "Let's get the book inside."

"Let him lay there," Perry said. "Pneumonia won't hurt him."

Coley got a firm grip on the man's shoulders, backed into the cellar inches at a time. He thought, those two will grab the loot for themselves. Why shouldn't I get some?

"He's like a ton of bricks," Coley said, "as long as he's paying for this, you can give me a hand."

Dawson hurried to help him and together they dragged the man close to the open furnace door. Fire licked sleepily out of a bed of coals inside the furnace. Coley removed his raincoat, dropped it across a table standing against the wooden ceiling support. He lay his helmet on the raincoat.

Perry said, "Make yourself at home. What did you mean when you made the crack about him paying for it?"

Coley hesitated. In the locker room down at the station house, that's all the boys talked about; the extra money the division men grabbed. Maybe they were wrong. "I know the score."

Dawson swung his felt hat, sent a spray against the stove. The sizzle sounded loud. A shrewd look in his eyes, he stared at Coley, said nothing.

Annoyed, Perry cried, "You speaking Greek or something?"

Dawson said, "We'd better get back to Block. He's got ten crap players—"

"He's got enough cops with him to run a precinct. You don't expect me to carry this book back to one hundred and forty-five?"

Coley said, "I can imagine you carrying him."

"You gonna answer me, Walsh? That's your name, isn't it?"

Coley sat down on the table corner. The table creaked in protest, threatening to collapse, but it held him. Coley took out a cigarette, lighted it, his hand trembling for an instant.

"There must be three grand in that black bag. What happens to that dough?"

Dawson said, "If the book can prove the money was not used in gambling, he can get it from the Police Property Clerk's Office. If he can't, the Police Pension Fund is gonna be a little richer."

Perry said, "We'll let the court worry about it, the court and the Police Legal Bureau."

The man on the floor sat up. He pushed his hat from his bushy brown head. Sweat and water and dirt ran down his face. His nose had bled, the blood drying in a smear around his lips.

Coley said, "Win or lose, he loses. If he wants to prove the money wasn't used in gambling, he's got to fight it in the Court. Which means he needs a mouthpiece who will grab himself a fat fee."

The man looked around him. "Time," he said thickly, "I lose a lot of time."

Perry said, "You got plenty time. I'm gonna see to it personally you spend a month in the hospital before you go to trial." His chin quivered with anger. "You knocked me over, up there in one hundred and forty-five, I won't forget that." Suddenly he kicked at the man's head, caught the side of the jaw. The man clutched at his face, his body turning halfway around.

Dawson cried, "Did you have to, Manny?"

The eyes deeply sunk in their sockets rolled restlessly. "Yeh, I had to."

Coley said, "The book will do business."

"Business? What's this business?"

"He wants the money back. The Property Clerk won't hand it over to him just like that."

Dawson said, "The book has to start an action in replevin in the Appellate Term. Then, maybe, he'll get the dough."

Coley said, "So he'll pay a lawyer a fancy fee and hope to God he wins."

Sunken eyes alert, Perry said, "Why don't you spit it out, Walsh?"

Dawson had an odd smile on his face. Hands dug deep in his pockets, he stood straddle-legged, the light of the furnace flames dancing in his eyes.

Coley said, "Ask the book if it ain't worth half the bag for us to save him all that fuss and bother."

Perry glared, breathing heavily. "Suppose it's worth it to him?"

Coley said, "He'd be happy to split the money with us."

Perry's voice was hoarse. "And for half that bag we forget we got him on a charge of maintaining a room for gambling, being a common gambler, assaulting an officer and escaping arrest?"

"That's your business. The money angle has nothing to do with the charges against him. You can still prosecute—"

Perry's hand shot out, grasped a handful of blue serge. "It's guys like you that give the department a black eye. For a couple bucks you'd sell us down the dirty river. I got a good mind to give you my knee right between your legs."

For an instant Coley's mind faltered. "What?" The color left his face. Slapping Perry's hand away from his blouse, he said. "Don't give me that crap. You're a division man. You grab what you can. You want the whole bag for yourself, don't you?"

Perry's voice shook. "Get out! Before I slam your damn face in, get out of here."

Dawson stepped between them, facing Coley. "Go on, son," he said softly. "He's not kidding."

Coley gave a brief, nervous smile. "He's trying to tell me—"

"He is telling you. That money will eventually go into the Police Pension Fund, every dime."

Moving in a half-daze, Coley picked up his helmet and raincoat. "I could use that dough, really use it ..."

Perry cried, "I'm gonna turn you in."

Dawson said, "No, you're not. He's just a kid who lost his head."

Perry sounded determined. "Cops like that we can do without."

Dawson took Coley's arm, led him to the door. "Tell the sergeant to send a wagon to the one hundred forty-five building and then to pick us up at this hole." He opened the door and a blast of wind slapped wetly against Coley's face.

Coley said, "I'll tell him."

Dawson squeezed his arm. "Don't worry, he won't blow the whistle on you."

Coley went outside, stood in the cold rain until his face grew numb, then walked slowly to the station house. When he got there, cold and soaking wet, he remembered his raincoat was still lying across his arm.

A week later the order came through on the teletype machine that Coley Walsh had been transferred to a new precinct. When informed, Coley breathed a sigh of relief.

Just a transfer. No fine. No suspension. No departmental trial. A transfer to the next precinct. Not up in the Bronx or out on Staten Island where a man could spend four hours a day coming and going to the job. Just another precinct, a new captain, a new lieutenant, new sergeants, new brother officers. Only the inspector was the same. Inspector Northern was in charge of three police precincts.

The following day as Coley entered the new precinct to change into the police uniform he kept in his locker, Patrolman Dawson slapped him on the back, said hello. In the lavatory, after glancing under the closed doors of the toilets to see if they were alone, Dawson said, "You think Perry got you heaved out of your precinct."

"If he did, it makes no sense. If he reported me to Northern—"

"He didn't."

"The transfer was coincidence?"

Dawson grinned smugly. "I got you transferred. You're the kind of a kid I would've liked to work with. You're sharp, you got something on the ball. Perry gives me a pain. I was figuring it was time him and me split up. Lots of times the inspector breaks up teams, maybe splitting up two hot rods and two creeps and pairing them up. Me and the inspector, we don't see eye to eye on a lot of things. If I asked for you, he'd get very suspicious. So I spoke to my friend Captain Wentigrid—"

"My new captain."

"—and told him what a partner you'd make for me."

Coley said, jubilantly, "I don't believe it. I'm gonna work in a division? Is that what you're telling me?"

Dawson smiled but there was sadness in his eye. "No, son, you're not going to work in a division on account of Captain Wentigrid needs a good precinct plainclothesman. In a day or so you'll get your new assignment as Captain Wentigrid's new bag man."

## Seven

Police Captain Wentigrid kept in shape by doing daily calisthenics. Ever since he had attended the gym classes in Delehanty's thirty-five years ago, Captain Wentigrid had exercised with ten-pound dumbbells before an open window. His muscular build belied his gray hair and fifty-six years. A member of the Rockaway Beach Polar Club, the captain found greatest comfort in a room when the windows were wide open, the radiators shut tight. Only when it rained or snowed fiercely would Captain Wentigrid condescend to partly close the windows.

Standing at ease before Captain Wentigrid, Coley waited for his new boss to look up from where he was writing on a yellow pad. Coley glanced at Ben Fields, sitting comfortably in a leather chair. Fields was to be Coley's partner, both assigned to Captain Wentigrid as his two precinct plainclothesmen. Fields was past forty-five, a red-faced man with a medicine-ball paunch.

Captain Wentigrid pushed the pad aside, looked up as if surprised to see the two men. "You two boys have a nice talk?"

"Yes, sir," Coley said. "It will be a pleasure working with Fields."

The captain looked up at Coley from under his bushy gray eyebrows. "I'm sure. Fields, does Walsh understand his duties?"

Fields nodded. "Walsh is quick to learn."

Captain Wentigrid lifted his shoulders in a shrug. "Then there is nothing for me to add." He gave Coley his hand. "Good luck, Walsh."

"Thank you, sir."

The captain picked up some memos from his desk.

"That bar on the avenue is bucking for a batch of summonses. Tell Birnbaum, any more complaints, I'll serve him personally."

Fields said to Coley, "Birnbaum pours rotgut into name brand whiskey bottles."

The captain said, "He's got to close by three o'clock on Sunday mornings, and if I get another mother complaining about her sixteen-year-old daughter being served liquor in Birnbaum's, he'll be one sorry guy. That Olson girl gets drunk and doesn't care with whom she sleeps. The mother is going to send the girl's doctor bills to the commissioner. Now these pushcart peddlers ..."

Within four weeks Coley handled the graft like a veteran. As he said to Fields, "You make a good teacher. For me it's like walking into an established business. All I got to know is from whom to collect and how much. We take a piece for ourselves and drop the rest of the take into the captain's desk drawer. The captain doesn't see us put it in, we don't see him take it out. I like this job."

However there were days when the job dulled with monotony, times when the doing of his duty gave Coley a funny feeling inside. Handing out summonses to itinerant pushcart peddlers brought the biggest grumbles.

"Slobs," he cried, "trying to keep off home relief."

Fields was sympathetic, but he explained that the rent-free peddlers were unfair competition to storekeepers.

Coley said sourly, "You don't see the division men doing this messenger boy work, petty arrests, handing out summonses for everything except spitting on the sidewalk, wasting a lot of time following up complaints sent in by cranks and revenge gangs. Give me excitement ..."

At times Coley got his excitement, for occasionally, on Inspector Northern's orders, Coley and his partner aided the shorthanded division men. Once they helped the division men in a raid on a giant still capable of producing hundreds of gallons of illegal alcohol daily. Another time they raided a Swedish masseur establishment which, as they'd known, turned out to be a bawdy house with suitable girls for the average thrill seeker. For those who desired other thrills, there were whips and chains.

"After that," Coley said, while they were having coffee in a restaurant, "I feel like I did a good day's work."

Fields chewed on a pizza. "You won't make a dime that way. I got bills to take care of. I don't bring a bundle for my wife to play with, she's the hardest person in the world to get along with. She loves money and what it'll buy."

Coley lighted a cigarette. "Everybody loves money. With it you're somebody, without it you can die in the streets."

"That polio specialist come yesterday?"

Coley nodded. "Billy is going to a private hospital this guy runs up in Riverdale. There, the kid will get the right personalized treatment. The doc didn't con me. Billy will never be a hundred per cent okay, but he says the leg will get stronger and the kid will be able to walk some day."

Fields was skeptical. "As long as there's money around you'll get plenty of hope."

A sudden sour taste in his mouth, Coley killed his cigarette in the tray. "We gotta keep punchin'. I'm making a nice dollar, might as well spend some of it on the kid. As long as those policy drops kick in with fifty a month, the bootleg liquor joints thirty, the gambling houses thirty-five and the bookies one hundred bucks on each and every month, besides what we grab not to make a pinch once in a while, I'll stay happy even if I spend every nickel of my take."

Fields laughed. "You won't be able to spend it all."

Coley finished his coffee. "I saw a nice place on Second Avenue. Five rooms, elevator apartment. Mom would like it."

Fields was startled. "Take it easy, Coley. You're not supposed to live in that kind of apartment, not on a cop's pay."

Coley shrugged. "Just talking, Ben ..."

Outside, they walked in silence for a few blocks, then standing opposite a barber shop, Fields squinted. "You see Spinelli in there?"

Coley nodded. "He's shaving."

Fields belched. "Every time I see him he's got lather on his face. Let's go collect one hundred bucks. If he bellyaches, I'm gonna tell him to go book in another precinct. We could get five hundred for his spot."

Spinelli handed Fields five twenty dollar bills. "Business ain't what it used to be. In the old days a guy could live it up."

Fields said. "You're still doing okay."

Spinelli's smile was forced. "In the old days we knew the score at every race track. Today we get no word which horse is out just for the ride and which horse is real hot. So the books get hit hard too often."

Fields opened the door. "The Syndicate is back in operation; maybe you can go back to the old days."

Spinelli shrugged. "It depends how much protection will cost." He rubbed his chin, a faraway look in his eyes. "Maybe it'll be a good deal."

Outside the wind pawed at their coats and whipped newspapers against their legs.

Coley's eyes narrowed against the wind. "What's with the Syndicate?"

Fields pulled up the collar of his coat. "You know in the old days the Syndicate ran most of the gambling in this town. Then they had to give it up: too much Mayor, too much Police Commissioner, too much honest cop."

"Things have changed?"

"Well, the pressure has kind of slackened. At least, the Syndicate thinks so. You know in most of the big towns, this same Syndicate has full control. Try to work in a cigar store or in a hotel or on a corner without the Syndicate's okay. And, I guess, the Syndicate's worth the cut they get. You get favors, small ones, big ones.

"They supply the mouthpiece for the book who gets pinched, they got better connections with the division men and the Commissioner's office and the Magistrates, so they can get a case heaved out. That's how it was in the old days. Maybe it'll come back to that. I don't know."

Coley cupped a pack of matches in his big hand, struck a match, moved the flame quickly to the cigarette. He blew smoke and the wind blew it back at him.

Coley said, "If the Syndicate's rolling in this town, how come I haven't heard about it?"

Fields studied a memo pad he'd pulled out of his pocket. "They've only started. Right now they accept voluntary members. Later, the rest will be forced in. They're playing it cute now. No rough stuff. Everything peaceful. A book joins, he can lay off big bets, the Syndicate will spread it out so if he gets hit, it'll be only for what he can afford to carry. The guys who don't join will find all of a sudden they're carrying big bets on hot horses and when they can't get rid of a big chunk of the bet, they lose their shirts. After that I'll bet he joins the Syndicate or the Combination or whatever fancy name they're using this time."

As they walked up the street the wind tore the cigarette out of Coley's mouth and sent it swirling into the gutter in a shower of sparks.

Coley watched the cigarette dance half across the gutter to find an opening in the sewer cover. "Who runs the Combo?"

"Dave Rodriguez runs the gambling end of it in

New York. He's a rough guy, not too smart but mean tough. Dave handles the gambling, the payoffs and collections. Right now he's got fifty juvenile delinquents working for him."

"Who's Dave's boss?"

"Henny Woods."

"That hop-head."

"He's smart, tough and a con man, a good combination for a man in charge of personnel of all the rackets in New York."

"I suppose he's got a boss too."

Fields nodded. "Guy called Pete Carlyle runs New York for the National Syndicate, the three or four big men who run every damn racket in this country. Carlyle himself stays out of the limelight."

Coley whistled. "Big shot Pete Carlyle."

Fields looked at him sidewise. "You know him?"

Coley didn't answer him and they walked in silence for two blocks. Abruptly, Coley stopped in his tracks. "Ben, we could make money, a lot of money."

"I'm satisfied."

"One year, two, and you could spit in the Commissioner's eye."

"Why should I spit in the Commissioner's eye?"

"You say the Syndicate is beginning to take on members?"

Fields counted on his bare fingers. "Cohen, Berman, DeLuca and Keavy in our precinct." He shoved his hands back into his coat pockets. "I don't know about the other precincts."

Coley slipped a cigarette between his lips. "Every choice spot except Spinelli's and Ryder's. Why do we let them?"

Fields was puzzled. "Let who?"

"For Chris' sakes, Ben, the Syndicate. Suppose we wanted to chase a guy out of the precinct; Spinelli, for instance. We lock him up a couple times and unless he's crazy and wants to get pinched every day, he'll move to another precinct. Right?"

"Why pick on Spinelli, he's paying off?"

Coley said angrily, "Take anybody. DeLuca, Cohen. We could give them the business and chase them out of here. Then where's the Syndicate's protection?"

Fields' eyes were fixed on the unlighted cigarette between Coley's lips. "In the old days the Syndicate could report to the beef man in the division and we'd be the ones to get shipped out of the precinct. Today ... well the Syndicate could get tough with us."

"They wouldn't dare without big brass behind them. Anyway, you said they wouldn't use rough stuff before they're completely organized."

Fields smiled. "I could be off on the time element. What's eating you, Coley?"

Coley squeezed Fields arm. "What's to stop us, you and me, from chasing every sonofabitch from the choice spots and putting in our own boys? We'd be the Syndicate for our own precinct. Why let somebody else horn in?"

Fields looked frightened. "Wait a minute, Coley. You telling me you wanna bank a dozen books?"

Fervently, Coley said, "You know damn well that's where the money is. We bank the game and pay off our boys on a percentage basis."

"Captain Wentigrid wouldn't like that one bit."

"We'll give him a cut and he'll be a happy man."

"He ain't that hungry to stick his neck out when he's got a sure thing now. You got enough money to back each book? Say ten grand for each and every book you get to work for you?"

Coley pulled the cigarette out of his mouth, crushed it. "That much?"

"Just about. The Syndicate places a couple big bets with your boys—after all, they're in with most of the horse owners and they know when a horse is on just for a workout or is going out to win. They could murder you with one good betting coup. Don't be a smart guy, Coley."

Coley flung the crushed cigarette into the wind. "I'm smarter than Rodriguez and that hop-hound who work for the Syndicate. Ben, how much can we scrape together?"

Fields shook his head. "You, not me. I make enough."

"I don't," Coley cried. "This is my chance to make it big. I'm taking it."

"Forty, fifty grand to start. You got that kind of dough?"

"I could start with half that. I got a couple grand. I think I could get twenty more. I'm gonna find out how peaceful that Syndicate really is."

That evening Coley sat drinking whiskey in the Cantor living room while for the third time Joseph Cantor apologized for Mille's absence.

A note of annoyance in his voice, Coley said, "I knew she was going out with Carlyle tonight. It's you I got business with. I got a good deal, only I need a partner with dough."

Cantor's eyebrows lifted. "This partner business, how much it costs me?"

Coley hesitated. "All you can do is refuse me, Pop. To run it right, fifty thousand bucks."

"My money and your brains?"

"We'll make a hundred grand in one year."

"With tips?"

Coley flushed. "Okay, I had it coming, I guess."

Cantor lifted his arms in a shrug. "All my life people come to Joe Cantor to do him a favor and make him a million dollars. What for I wanna be a millionaire? Me, my wife, we got plenty money to leave to charity when we die."

Squirming in his seat, Coley said, "This is a good investment. You didn't even ask what it was."

Cantor slapped his forehead. "Fifty thousand dollars! You know what you ask? You want a thousand, Coley, you got it. You give it back in ten years. Pay me a dime a week."

"I could get going with forty grand."

"Two thousand I give you."

"Twenty grand."

"Three thousand, Coley. I love you like a stepson."

Coley stood up. "Don't you want to listen to my proposition?"

Cantor said, "For a man to make a fortune overnight, the proposition got to be crooked. Better I don't hear it."

Coley said, "It's a good deal, as good as anything you ever invested in, but if you don't want to hear it, I can't force you."

Pleading, he said, "You want five thousand dollars? I worked hard for my money; blood and sweat …"

"This money you'll make a lot easier."

"A dollar and a half a day I made …"

"I get the point, Pop."

Cantor's forehead creased. "I want my wife and I, we should never want for anything. Coley, if I listen to all my friends who got good propositions, I have to go back to work on a sewing machine."

Coney opened the door. "Okay, I got my answer. Stop looking so glum. It's your dough, Pop. So long …"

Ben Fields wasn't sympathetic on hearing Coley's story. Sitting in a restaurant, half-filled cups of coffee before them, Fields said, "You sure had a lot of gall."

"I know, but the idea was so good, I had to make a try. That Pop's a nice guy. Even when he says no, you know he's really sorry." Coley dropped a lighted match into his coffee and listened to the sizzle as the red tip turned black, the match floating in the coffee.

"Ben, I think I can get into the Syndicate, but I'll need your help."

"Don't look at me."

"Once I get into that organization, you come in with me."

"I'm satisfied on my measly two grand extra pay a month."

"The Syndicate's got six of our books tied."

"Seven. Flynn joined them yesterday."

"I'm gonna push those boys around a little. Flynn, Cohen, the seven of 'em. I'm chasing them off their spots and putting other men in their place."

Fields' complexion paled. "You talk from fever."

Coley's face was set, determined. "We chased guys before. We sold a good spot to Flynn for a grand."

"That was different. Gollen was giving us trouble, so we had to chase him. Captain Wentigrid didn't care one way or the other."

Coley said, "He wouldn't care, not if his take was the same. The captain never asks questions, not as long as we drop his regular bundle into his desk drawer."

"I don't like it. Those boys are nice guys."

"Nice guys wind up in the craphouse. Seven lousy guys out of one-forty under contract. I need this break, Ben."

Fields crushed the check in his hand, rolled it into a ball. "For your own benefit, I should say no."

Sharply, Coley said, "I don't need tears."

"Why you trying to get the Syndicate riled up? That is your purpose, isn't it?"

Coley opened Fields' clenched fist, took out the check, opened it flat on the table, tried to press out the creases.

"Ben, give me one month to try out my plan. If it doesn't work, those seven boys get their spots and nobody's hurt too much. To make up your mind, Ben, I'll give you an extra five hundred out of my take."

Fields drew his thin lips into a tight line.

"Goddamn it, Coley," he said, "you can be an insulting bastard. I don't want your dough."

"What do you want, Ben?"

"Just leave me alone."

"Tomorrow I work on Cohen; he's first."

Fields put both hands on the table, pushed himself up. "Just keep me out of this, Coley. Anything you do is on your own." He dropped a bill on the table. "I won't interfere ... unless I'm forced to."

Coley said, "Keep the money; I'm paying the check." But Fields was out of the restaurant.

Hymie Cohen was short and squat, restless dark eyes in a florid face. When he spoke he got up on his toes as if to get closer to Coley's ear.

"I didn't give you an accommodation arrest last week?"

"It's you I'm lockin' up this time."

"Tomorrow, I'll get a stand-in."

"You, Hymie, not some goddamn kid."

Hymie blinked. "I don't get it. You're kidding Little Hymie?"

Coley spat a mouthful of gum into the gutter. "I'm locking you up now, tomorrow, the day after."

"Why?" Hymie cried. "Why you persecutin' me? I don't pay my ice?"

"We just want you out of the precinct."

Tears came into Hymie's eyes. "What are you, a undertaker? I been working this spot for ten years."

"You don't own this corner."

"I paid enough ice to own the whole block. I ain't taking this on my back."

Coley grasped a handful of coat and shirt. "You little sonofabitch, who you talking to, one of your damn friends?"

Cohen trembled. "You're taking the bread out of my kids' mouths. I go out of this precinct, I start from scratch. Here, I know everybody. You figurin' on setting up somebody in this spot?"

"That's none of your business."

"Lemme buy this spot back. How much?"

Coley pushed Hymie away. "We want you out. No reason, nothing personal, just out."

The tears threatened to overflow. "Where'm I gonna go? A guy's got a right to work. The law says so."

Coley looked up and down the quiet street. "Tell it to the Syndicate."

A horrified look in his eyes, Hymie said, "The Syndicate is doing this, huh, Walsh? Tell me the truth, they're the ones shoving me out."

Coley slipped a Chiclet between his teeth and looked wise.

Hymie cried, "Imagine that! I join 'em and they do this."

"I didn't say that, Hymie."

"I'll tell that goddamn Rodriguez. Him and his lousy friends are taking over, that's what they're trying to do. I won't let 'em get away with it."

"Let's go, Hymie."

"All right, all right. Look, Walsh, I can take a hint. Tomorrow I don't come back here. So what's the sense pinching me today?"

Coley took Hymie's arm. "Just to impress it on your mind, I'll give you a break when I'm making out the complaint in the Gamblers' Court. I'll just say I saw you make a couple bets and your confession: 'Please, officer, I was doing this for only a couple years.'"

Hymie groaned. "You're crucifyin' me, Walsh. What I ever done to you?"

That afternoon in Magistrate's Gamblers' Court, Cohen pleaded guilty to the crime of possessing policy slips. The Magistrate fixed bail of five hundred dollars and set a day for sentence. Pale and shaken, Cohen slunk out of the courtroom. Coley went to look for Flynn, his second victim. Within two weeks seven men who had joined the Syndicate were banished, and new men, working on less lucrative corners in the precinct, paid five hundred dollars each for the privilege of taking over the vacant spots. Coley tossed half the take into Captain Wentigrid's desk drawer. Now everybody would be happy, everybody but the Syndicate and its members.

## Eight

The Desk Sergeant's brown eyes blinked out of a coarsely freckled face. He leaned over the docket book, a lock of gray hair dropping over his right eye.

"Give me that name again, Walsh. Lately I'm kind of hard of hearing."

Bored, Coley said to the pimply-faced young man with the bleached red hair and soft full mouth. "You give it to him."

The young man lifted a handkerchief to his nose, and when he pulled it away the handkerchief was stained red. "Marilyn Monroe," he said distinctly. "Those nasty boys made my nose bleed."

Coley said to the sergeant, "He solicited the wrong kids. In the men's room of the Independent Subway. The kids banged him around a little. When we got there, they were trying to flush his head down a toilet bowl."

The young man waved a hand. "I almost drowned. Nasty boys."

Coley said, "Give the sergeant your right name or I'll do what those kids did, and there'll be nobody to save you."

The man said, "My name is Marilyn Monroe. Ask anybody on Eighth Avenue."

The desk sergeant said, as he wrote, "Marilyn Monroe."

The man's mascaraed blue eyes smiled triumphantly. "See, even the sergeant knows I'm

Marilyn Monroe."

Coley said, "Make it a section eight, Sarge."

The sergeant said, "Subdivision eight. Section eight is for the army locos."

Coley said, "This guy is no different."

The man took a lipstick holder and a mirror out of his corduroy jacket pocket. Coley slapped them out of his hand.

"You're gonna look like a man even if you're not."

The young man laughed a sweet indulgent laugh. "Sticks and stones don't bother me."

Coley spied Ben Fields coming out of the captain's office. A detective coming down the stairs said something to Fields, then hurried out the back way. Fields came over, a smile on his face.

"Donovan's wife is out front waiting to grab his pay."

Coley laughed. "Donovan's girl friend is out in the back."

The sergeant lifted his head from the book. "This your collar, Walsh?"

"I'll take it," Fields said.

Coley nodded. "Okay with me. After he's booked, Ben, meet me out front."

The prisoner booked and lodged in the station house cell, Fields came outside to find Coley leaning against the stoop. It was a cool evening, a full moon in a star-spangled sky.

Coley took a last puff on a cigarette, tossed it into the gutter. "C'mon, I'll show you a dream."

They turned the corner. At the curb stood a shiny new convertible, its swift, sleek lines of blue and red emphasizing its breath-taking beauty.

Coley said, "Nifty, isn't it?"

Fields stared at Coley until realization dawned on him. "This car isn't yours?"

"You wanna bet?" Coley took his key ring out of his pocket, leaned over the door handle. The car door flew open.

"Get in," Coley said, "I'll ride you home. Pipe that inside, blue and red. All I do is push buttons. I got power brakes that can stop me on a dime. You like white wall tires?"

Fields blinked in stunned amazement. "Damn it, Coley, what did I tell you about showing off your money?" His forehead wrinkled. "You bought it on the installment plan, I hope."

Coley waved him down. "Don't hope so much. It was one of those things, Ben. Somebody I know, an old-time bootlegger, Tony Madera, went broke in a crap game. He needed money quick so he offered me the car for twenty-five hundred cash. How the hell could I pass up this steal? The car's brand new, less than a thousand miles. It's got a heater, radio—get in, Ben, and see for yourself."

Ben Fields seemed rooted to the spot. "Where does a cop get twenty-five hundred for a car? Coley, you're sticking your neck out. And you got Captain Wentigrid and me out on the same rotten limb. What the hell gets into you? If the Captain ever got wind of this—"

Coley said quickly, "That's why I didn't park it near the station house. Ain't she a beauty, Ben? These Cadillacs run like purring kittens."

Anger in back of his blue eyes, Fields said, "Sell it quick. You hear me, Coley? Get rid of it before some cop we know reports you riding in this battle wagon."

Coley looked away. "Don't worry bout it. You gonna get in?"

"No," he snapped. "I never saw you with a Caddy convertible. Just get rid of it by tomorrow."

Coley's voice was cool, controlled. "I got to have it, Ben."

"You've got marbles in your head."

"Shut up, Ben." He bit his teeth hard, the jaw muscles forming hard ridges. Slowly, he relaxed. "You don't want to ride with me, say so. Don't give me any more arguments."

"Coley, listen to me." Ben Fields held Coley by his coat lapels.

Coley shrugged him off. "I like this car. I'm gonna keep it." He slipped into the seat. "You comin'?"

Fields wheeled and stalked down the street. Coley watched him go, wishing he hadn't talked so sharply. Ben was a nice guy.

When Fields vanished around the corner, Coley slammed the door closed. He rolled down the windows but before he could start the motor a soft, singsong voice said, "Hey, Walsh, maybe we can talk, *si?*"

Coley stuck his head out and looked up at a big brown man with shiny white teeth in a bronzed face. The man smiled, full of good humor, vaseline glistening on his small mustache. This was Dave Rodriguez.

Coley said, "What you want?"

A grin, a shrug. "You snap my head to pieces."

"I got no business with you, Rodriguez.

Dark eyes alert, Rodriguez said, "My boys, they are having a little bit trouble with you."

"Your boys, Rodriguez? You the big boss?"

The smile was gone. "Okay, Syndicate boys. Let me tell you, Walsh, this Syndicate, it is one tough outfit."

Coley laughed. "Those days are gone, Rodriguez. Anyway, I don't give a good damn."

Rodriguez touched the car as he leaned his big body over to whisper. "Maybe you want to make couple dollars, Walsh?"

Coley said, "Get your hand off the car. Rodriguez, I'm a cop and I'll pinch any bookie I catch."

Rodriguez' thick lips curled. "How much, cop?"

"Move, Rodriguez, before I run your goddamn legs over."

Rodriguez softened his tone. "What you want, Walsh? There must be reason you pick on Syndicate books? What you want, maybe I get it for you."

Coley started the motor. "Tell your boss, Henny Woods, I don't understand your English."

Rodriguez pleaded. "Ride me uptown. Five minutes—"

"This ain't a cab."

The car pulled slowly away from the curb. Chuckling, Coley leaned back in his car. Finally, after a full week during which Coley was beginning to think the Syndicate wouldn't contest the upheaval of their gambling power in Captain Wentigrid's precinct, Rodriguez had come. Now there'd be some action, one way or the other.

That Tuesday, after spending most of the day checking minor complaints and handing out summonses, Coley was called to aid Inspector Northern's division men in a raid on a floating crap game. It was almost midnight when, the raid successfully accomplished, Coley headed for home. It was a cool night, the dampness searching his flesh through his clothing, the voice of the pending storm a sullen howling in the distance.

Tired, hungry, Coley hurried his step down Rivington Street. He saw the man leaning up against the black sedan but too sleepy to think, Coley passed the car. Something vague clicked in his head. He turned to glance back but the man was on him, swinging something shiny. Coley tried to duck away. The sky came down on his head exploding into a million dirty lights.

A voice, thick and unrecognizable, came from a mile away. "In the alley. Don't mark up his face. Just give him something to remember us by."

Hands tugged at him, dragged him over the pavement.

"Okay," the voice said, "and make it fast and snappy."

The kick in the ribs drove the wind out of Coley. He rolled, gasping, got to his feet.

"Give it to him," the voice cried, "He's got a cannon."

On rubber legs Coley swung out at a blurred form shuffling in on him. The form sank to the concrete. Coley reached for his revolver just as a husky man slammed into him in a football tackle, knocking him completely off his feet. Coley sat up and somebody kicked him in the face.

"Don't mark him, just learn him a lesson he won't forget. You listenin', cop? You got a job, stick to it. Butt into our business again and we'll kill you dead. Let's go."

Blows rained on him, beating him down to his knees by the very fury of the attack. Coley kept punching, but the fists came faster, then the kicks, driving him into the soft comforting darkness.

Somebody was shaking him and he felt wet, as if he'd dozed off on the stringpiece and fallen into the river with his clothes on. Coley lay there, not opening his eyes, wondering why his body was full of pain. Then, remembering, he sat up, a groan escaping his lips. The rain was coming down in a fine drizzle.

A man said, "You all right, mister? I sent my wife to get a policeman."

Coley pushed the man away, struggled to his hands and knees, pulled himself erect with the aid of the brick wall.

Coley didn't recognize his voice. "I don't need a policeman. I'm okay."

The man said, "I saw them beating you from my car. Four of them."

"Go home." Coley brushed rain from his face. "Look, mister, thanks for your trouble. Those men were friends of mine. It was a private argument. Now get out of my way."

Coley couldn't sleep. The pain was bearable now, and except for the bruised cheek and torn lower lip, he was unmarked. What bothered him most of all was his stupidity. Had he not known that the Syndicate had two choices? They could try to buy him off or try to stop him cold. Knowing that, he should have been on guard.

From now on, he resolved, they'd never catch him without a gun in his fist and if somebody died and the Commissioner asked questions, then this would be another case where a stick-up had been attempted on the wrong guy.

Toward morning, thinking of Mom's startled look when he'd come into the house, the way her lips curled in derision when he'd explained how he'd fallen down a flight of stairs, he fell asleep.

When he awoke he was stiff all over, as if muscles he'd never used had been overworked. Mom already had the coffee up when he appeared in his pajamas.

"Mom," Coley said, "call up the precinct and report me sick. Then get my partner Fields on the phone."

"What should I tell them?"

"I told you, I fell down the stairs, but I'll be okay by tomorrow."

Without telling Fields what had happened, Coley learned that Dave Rodriguez lived in a renovated elevator apartment house on Avenue A. By ten o'clock, Coley was in the Avenue A corner candy store, searching the telephone book for Rodriguez' telephone number. After a while, he went into the booth and made his call.

Rodriguez' gruff voice said, "*Hola?*"

"Dave? This is Coley Walsh."

There was a pause. "Yes, what is?"

"I was thinking about that talk I had with you last week. I want to talk again with you."

Rodriguez had a chuckle in his tone. "Maybe you

changed your mind about my boys?"

Coley forced a laugh. "Maybe. I've got a right to change my mind if I want to."

"*Si, si*," Rodriguez was very happy. "All of a sudden?"

"Frankly, I met a couple guys and they convinced me maybe I made a mistake. You know, every day we learn something new. Can we talk?"

"I think about it."

Coley said, "Think fast; I still got your boys out in the cold."

Rodriguez seemed to be considering this. "Hokay," he said, "you come up and we make talk."

"I can't afford to have your wife see me."

Rodriguez was insulted. "I don't talk business in front of her. Anyways, my wife, she is visiting with a neighbor."

Dressed in a blue silk robe, Rodriguez opened the door for Coley. A smirk twisted Rodriguez' lips as he watched Coley step into the large overly-furnished apartment. Coley walked through the living room, glancing over the variety of bright colors.

Rodriguez, impatient, said, "I got business outside."

Coley faced him. "You got tough boys working for you. Gotta give you credit. You're sure on the job, sending those four men to talk to me."

Hands in his robe pockets, Rodriguez preened himself. "I do my job."

Quietly, Coley said, "I thought it was you responsible for my workout. I wanted to be sure."

Instantly alert, Rodriguez said, "What you mean?"

"Those boys taught me one thing. Never trust a damned crook."

The cords on Rodriguez' neck stood out like ropes. "You be careful what you say, Walsh."

Mockingly, Coley bowed. "Sure I will. Do me a favor? Take a message back to your boss. After I get through booting out every Syndicate bookie in my precinct, I'm going to get help from cop friends in adjoining precincts to do the same. I'm going to dent the Syndicate so bad it'll be a long time recovering."

Rodriguez' face was full of torment. "Next time you get worked out so good you don't never walk again."

Coley grasped a handful of robe and pulled Rodriguez close. "You'll have to do better than that." Cold anger thickened his voice. "You'll have to kill me because, so help me God, if anybody ever lays a hand on me again, I'm gunning for you, then Woods, then your big boss, Carlyle. Even if I got to do it on crutches. Tell that to your bosses for me."

Rodriguez' lips became slack, his dark eyes moving erratically, "Don't get so excited. I tell them, I tell them."

Coley smiled. "I want you to show them proof I mean every word I say. Here's a sample."

In a quick movement, he brought up his knee. Rodriguez gasped, clutched his groin, his face a sickly hue. As Rodriguez was keeling over, Coley drove his knee into the man's head. The big man dropped with a thud that shook the room. Coley kicked him twice in the ribs and when the man began to vomit, spit at him and went out of the apartment.

Coley drove home and this time slept peacefully and soundly. When he awoke at eight o'clock in the evening, he felt completely refreshed. After two ham sandwiches and two cups of coffee, completely content, Coley decided to go for a ride to Brooklyn.

Mille had Peter Carlyle for company.

Not stopping in the doorway, Coley said, "Didn't know you were busy, doll. Hi, Pete."

Mille lifted her eyebrows, watched Coley sit down. "Why don't you come in, Mr. Walsh?"

Carlyle studied Coley's bruised face. "A cop's life must be tough at times."

"Oh, I don't know," Coley laughed. "There are compensations, not necessarily the money kind. How's business, Pete?"

Carlyle shrugged. "Do you really care?"

"Sure. Who knows, maybe someday I might join you in one of your enterprises."

Carlyle took a cigar out of his pocket, fumbled with the wrapper. "That cut on the lip," he said, "should have had a stitch."

Smooth, cool fingers under his chin, Mille lifted Coley's head. "How did this happen?"

Coley spoke to Carlyle. "I stepped on somebody's toes and a bunch of goons caught me off guard. They won't catch me off guard again, I promise you. Next time there'll be a couple of corpses in the gutter."

Carlyle lighted his cigar, puffed hard. "If this was not official police duty wouldn't you have some explaining to do?"

Coley leaned forward in his chair. "I wouldn't be the first cop some bums tried to mug. If the Commissioner investigates, maybe the whole story will come out. I'll be in a jam but those muscle men, and their bosses, will have a bit of trouble. I'll take my chances."

Carlyle had admiration in his eyes. "You've got courage, Coley."

"Where I was brought up, the kids learn early in life if somebody pushes you, push back to keep from winding up down the sewer."

Sincerely, Carlyle said, "A good philosophy. I admire you."

Coley took the drink Mile held out. "Your admiration and a token will get me into the subway."

Carlyle got up. His eyes wise and friendly, he said, "If I were a subway agent, I might let you in without a token. Mille, I've got to run along. I'll pick you up

Friday. This time I'll bring a box of anti-seasick pills." His handshake was firm and he pumped Coley's hand a little longer than necessary. "I'll see you again, Coley."

After he'd gone, Mille sat down on the couch, facing Coley. "That cat-and-mouse conversation you had with Peter, is it secret, or can I ask questions?"

Coley moved over to the couch. "Ask all you like, you'll get no answers from me. You going on a cruise with Carlyle?" When she nodded, he felt a jealous pang. "That should be very cozy."

Her smile faded. "You making double-talk again, Coley?"

He shrugged helplessly. "I'm just sorry it's not me who had a yacht. I'd take you out to a desert island and I'd tell the captain to come back for us in a year."

Mille laughed. "Nine months is long enough."

He pulled her to him, kissed her cheek, her chin, her mouth. "Tell Carlyle to take a trip around the world, alone."

Her eyes roamed over his face. "Why should I tell him, Coley?"

"You know damn well why."

"Tell me, I want to hear you."

"I love you, baby, I love you so bad thinking of you and Carlyle out on his damned boat gives me pains in the chest." He kissed her fiercely and suddenly her arms were around his neck.

"I love you, Coley, I love you," she whispered. "I love you more than anything in the world."

He smothered her mouth with his lips and the heat swept over him, a tingling warmth that ran up from his loins and down from his belly.

"Don't, Coley." Her sharp tone belied the look in her eyes.

He dug his teeth into her neck. With a sweeping motion, he pulled at her blouse and it came away in his hand.

Sitting in a straight-backed chair, he watched her through the smoke screen, her legs stretched out comfortably, her head resting on the back of the club chair.

Coley said, "You're sorry."

She leaned her head forward and there was a kind of radiance shining from her face.

"No, darling, I'm not sorry. I hope I never will be."

"You won't," he said positively. "Now you're part of me. That's how I feel. I've got something good and sweet and it's all mine and nobody in the world is gonna take it away from me, God or nobody else. You understand what I'm saying?"

She nodded and smiled.

His voice throbbed. "From now on your nights belong to me. No more Carlyle, no more damn buyers. Cantor doesn't like it, quit him."

Gently she said, "I don't intend to quit my job until after we're married."

Coley stared stupidly. "Married?"

"You know what the word means. When two people are in love."

He ran his hand through his hair. "I know, sure I know. Don't rush me."

The slow flush came up from her chest, spreading unevenly over her face. "I'm sorry, Coley. Shotguns went out of style years ago. I just thought ..." She moved her hands in a helpless gesture. "I said a dirty word and I'm sorry."

Coley tried to take her hand but she moved away. He pleaded, "Mille, you don't understand."

"Right now I don't think you could make me understand."

He pulled her to him. "One thing you've got to get straight: I love you with all my heart. But this marriage business, it came so suddenly. Mille, I got burned once."

Eyes flashing, she cried, "I might be Francine the second. After all I'm a model and everybody knows about models."

He protested fiercely. "It isn't that at all. It's just that my dumb brain is in a damned rut and I need a little time to get it out."

She looked him in the eye. "All right, Coley. Please go home. I have a headache."

"Don't go on that boat ride with Carlyle. He's not for you."

She twisted away from him. "But you are? You know something, Coley, in some ways he's better for me, a lot better than you."

"What the hell do you know about the guy?"

"More than he suspects. I'm not a fool, Coley. He's a legitimate businessman; Peter has stocks and bonds and towel supplies and real estate. And then there's the big black car that follows him around wherever we go. So Peter's hands are a little soiled. Have you looked at your hands lately?"

"I was just getting the record straight, that's all. I don't pretend I'm Honest Coley Walsh. I just didn't want you putting Carlyle up on a pedestal."

She said, "Peter is an important man and I like him up on a pedestal. He belongs there."

Hoarsely, he cried, "Someday I'll be up there too, right up on top. See if I don't ... don't be mad at me, baby."

She shrugged. "I'm not mad at you. It isn't your fault. I just assumed too much." Her voice was sharp. "Just don't tell me what I can or can't do, Coley."

"I'll call you ..."

She sounded listless. "Do that, Coley."

## Nine

Henry Woods was waiting for Coley outside the precinct two days later.

Coley saw a man with Dave Rodriguez against a stoop across the street. Rodriguez nodded and jerked his head in Coley's direction, then the man crossed the gutter. Coley permitted him to catch up on the corner.

The man said in a raspy voice. "I'm Henny Woods. You, I understand, are Coley Walsh."

Henny Woods was built like a wrestler, thick-set and somewhat short. His bloated face was flat and dull. When he spoke, he looked at a spot on Coley's tie as if lifting his head higher would be an ordeal.

"Walsh, how about coming over to my apartment for a couple drinks?"

Coley looked at his wrist watch. "I'm busy."

Woods' smile was bland, genial. "I won't be available again, I promise you. As it is, I went out of my way to say hello."

"Okay," Coley said. "I can spare an hour or so."

Woods said dryly. "Thanks, Walsh."

Coley gave him a quick look. There was no trace of expression on the man's face. Coley felt a vague annoyance, as if Woods were laughing at him.

Henny Woods lived in a four-room apartment on West Fifty-fifth Street. Expensively furnished, the living room was crowded with massive pieces of furniture. Three club chairs and a giant-size couch were separated by shiny mahogany end tables, a coffee table, credenza and a fireplace. The table lamps were so tall they threatened to topple at a whisper. Brocade drapes and thick multicolored carpeting fitted in with the generally overcrowded appearance of the room.

A glass of Scotch in his hand, Coley relaxed in a club chair and waited for Woods to finish his whispered conversation with a big man who'd met them downstairs. A whine in his voice, the man was pleading for some kind of job. Woods kept shaking his head. Once his voice rose a notch.

"The boss says you're out. You can't make a living running numbers, get into some other business. We can't use you ... once was enough ... Okay, so you lost your head ... we can't use guys who can't keep cool ..."

Coley studied the man's coarse features. Somewhere, Coley knew, he'd met this man. He tried to recall the when and wherefore and, failing, it annoyed him.

After a while the man went out, still whining, and Woods closed the door after him.

"Sorry, Walsh ... another drink?" When Coley shook his head, Woods sat down opposite him. An amused look in his eyes, Woods said, "Walsh, you could've come here with your proposition 'stead of pushing my boys around."

Coley stirred in his seat. "I was under the impression you were the one with the proposition."

Woods' lower lip twitched with disdain. "Let's get one thing straight, Walsh. Having you here isn't my idea. If it was up to me I'd get you out of our hair, one way or another."

"Maybe your boss is smarter than you."

Woods scowled. "And maybe he ain't. You chased Syndicate boys, and nobody else, out of your precinct. And the only reason I can think of is—shakedown."

Coley laughed. "Think what you like. The truth is, I decided to set up my own syndicate. I got backing to work kvery bookie joint in my precinct. Once we start making money, I'll spread out into other precincts. Eventually, my boys will own New York."

Disbelief wrinkled Woods' face. "You gonna sit there and tell me some crummy outfit is buckin' the Syndicate?"

"Why the hell not?"

"We're too strong. We could knock off your books inside of a month with a couple good bets. You know that."

"Give me my hat and coat and I'll forget I was here."

Woods waved him down. "I wish to hell you would. In fact, just give me a good reason to heave you out."

Coley said, "You give me a reason and I'll spit in your face."

They stared at each other with harsh, chill distrust.

Then Woods got up, took a half-turn around the room. "I've got a proposition for you. I was told to put you on the payroll for one hundred bucks a week."

Coley snapped. "You sure you boys can spare it?"

"One-fifty and that's as high as we'll go. You work with Rodriguez, and answer to him."

"Now I got me a rotten boss."

Woods blew into his fist, his beady eyes staring at Coley's tie. Coley felt a vague unease as he wondered if he was overplaying his hand.

Woods said, "Take the job for three months. If you make good you'll get another fifty a week. If you don't, we'll fire you, and the hell with your backers."

"I'm not dropping my cop's job—"

As if the talk had palled on him, Woods said, "If you weren't a cop, we couldn't use you."

Coley laughed to hide his confusion. "Draw me a map."

"We need new members, new books, new numbers collectors, in our organization. You're gonna get 'em for us. The more you get to join us, the bigger your pay is gonna get. No rough stuff, just good salesmanship. They need us, we need them. You can do it; you got the personality, the mouthpiece and the brains. So I was told. I want every book in your precinct to come in with us. And when you're finished in your precinct, you'll move on to the precincts around you. Your badge should help a lot meeting people and convincing them. Maybe you can get a division man or even a lieutenant to work with you in the other precincts. The first thing tomorrow, my boys go back to their spots, Cohen, Flynn, all of them."

"What's the difference, your boys or mine, providing they join the Syndicate?"

Woods shook his head. "My boys go back, the word goes around: The Syndicate takes care of their own, and if anything goes wrong the Syndicate has the power to straighten things out. That alone will get us new members. You'll have a free expense account, within reason. I don't have to tell you to use your head. Some precincts you might not be able to touch ..."

Coley smiled, "Like you said, let me use my judgment."

Woods said without raising his voice, "Since I was a kid I never trusted a cop, especially a crooked one. I think you got bright ideas, Walsh. Don't practice them on me."

Coley got up. "You got me all wrong, Henny."

Henny's eyes were lustreless. "If I have, I'll apologize. My boys will be around you all the time. Just don't forget that."

Coley shrugged. "You're a stubborn guy, Henny. That man that came in with us, the panhandler we met out in the hall ..."

"He's no panhandler. He used to work for me but he's got a hot head and before he gets us in a jam, I sent him back to running numbers. Why you asking?"

"I thought I knew him."

"Jimmy Luckman?"

Coley smiled. "I knew somebody looks like him. So long, Henny."

Cantor was surprised when he opened the door that evening and found Coley standing in the doorway. "Coley! Come in, come in. Make a *shnapps*."

"Not this time, Pop. I saw a guy today who looked familiar to me. I'm talking about Jimmy Luckman,

Pop, the guy who tried to cut you up in your office."

Cantor's mouth screwed up. "Him! That dirty dog."

"Maybe I can help you, Pop."

Cantor sat down on a club chair. "Luckman don't bother me no more. Now I got a new headache. A Spanish guerrilla."

Coley stood over Cantor. "What does he look like?" Cantor shrugged. "Big like a giant, a mustache that shines like a neon light ..."

Coley mused. So they had Rodriguez in on the shakedown now.

Coley sat down, his eyes level with Cantor's. "What do they want?"

Cantor sighed, looked away. "My blood. They want I should sell them a piece of my business. Twenty-five per cent of Cangro for fifteen thousand dollars."

Coley shook his head in puzzlement. "The shares are worth more than the fifteen thousand dollars?"

Cantor slapped his hands together. "Shares can be worth fifteen thousand and they can be worth nothing. Pieces of paper. If I ask they should give me twenty thousand dollars, they give me. More maybe."

Coley cried, "Then what's the beef? They're not stealing—"

"Not now, later." Cantor jumped up. "Now they buy twenty-five per cent. A couple months, I got a little trouble with my workers or maybe somebody drops acid on my garments and I find Luckman and his gangsters will fix everything for another twenty-five per cent. One year and I got no more business. All my life I work and build up a suit and dress house and the gangsters, they got it. No sweat, no blood, just a little money invested. These gangsters buy in a lot of business houses; dresses, suits and cloaks, buttons, millinery, hats."

Coley said. "If they buy twenty-five per cent, you're

still boss."

Cantor said exasperatedly, "You're a child. I'm boss? I can push them out? They are gangsters. They get one finger inside my door, I gotta make room for a hand. So I sell twenty-five per cent. Then my new partner marches around the place like a Cossack. He bothers my workers. I get tough, so the next day the size tags are mixed up on my garments and I got trouble from every retail store. Maybe I get a truck hijacked."

Coley said, "So you get so disgusted you sell out for peanuts."

"I got to run like a plague is after me," Cantor cried, slapping his knees. "Who needs it? So far the union and me, we get along. But suppose these gangsters get their crooks into the International? Suppose they organize their own 'paper' union? Strikes! Every week strikes. So how can I stop a strike? By giving my partner another ten per cent, and another and another. Soon I get pushed out by the Board of Directors my partners appointed; out in the street with nothing on my back."

Coley whistled noiselessly for a second. "You go to the cops and give them the story and they can't do a thing. Somebody offered you a price for a piece of your business. That's no crime."

Cantor laughed harshly. "So I will tell the police that sometimes my carts get hit by a truck and the dresses fall in the mud. Or one of my trucks is robbed from a couple hundred dollars dresses or some *shnook* in the factory starts trouble. I got proof who and what and where? I know, but that means something in court?"

"Then these dress houses undersell you until you're crawling on your belly. So they lose for a while. Hell, they got rackets to make it up on. When your tongue is hanging out the Syndicate steps in and buys your outfit for a song."

Tiredly Cantor said, "I'm getting too old to fight."

## Ten

A somber quiet hung over Water Street. The last cold breath of winter made the blood thicken and tingle. A pigeon swooped down into the gutter, fluttered to a stop in the circle of light made by the lamppost in the middle of the street. In a moment another pigeon joined it. They strutted side by side, heads bobbing.

As Coley crossed the cobblestoned gutter, the pigeons took off in a flurry of silver wings. Coley stopped in front of the yellow brick warehouse, glanced up and down the deserted street before knocking on the thick wood door. A four-inch square of wood in the door opened at eye level. Two black eyes looked out at Coley.

"*Hola*," the man said, swinging open the door.

Coley said, "Hi, Pedro, you still knockin' up the broads?"

"Once in a while," Pedro laughed.

Hugging the damp brick wall, Coley went up a flight of narrow wooden steps, to where light illuminated the second floor landing. Men in shirtsleeves sat hunched around a long rectangular table. Empty coffee containers littered the floor. Crumpled cardboard boxes, some still containing sandwiches, lay on the table. The men didn't lift their eyes from where they worked, the pay-off slips, yellow bookkeeping papers listing the names of horses, hockey and basketball games, the amounts wagered, and the winners, holding their complete attention. Half a dozen ball-point pens, a dozen sharpened pencils, a copy of the *Morning Telegraph*, a *National Program*, two copies of the *Racing Form* and a copy of *Davey Sports Bulletin* were scattered over the table.

It was quiet except for the rustle of the paper and the clicking of the six tabulating machines.

Lighting a cigarette, Coley pushed open a glass-partitioned door at the end of the floor. Dave Rodriguez, hair glistening under the naked electric bulb hanging over his head, was working on tally sheets. Face dark and sullen as he stopped to look around at Coley, he muttered something unintelligible.

Coley said, "I hooked a division lieutenant from the eighth to work with me. He'll swing plenty into our organization."

"What about the ninth?"

"No dice," Coley said sitting down on a wooden chair. "But I got a cop who'll feel around and get the lay of the land."

Rodriguez toyed with a pencil. "It don't come in fast enough."

Coley shrugged. "You can't rush things. I got you over fifty new members."

"That Henny," Rodriguez grunted. "He make me crazy."

"He's sore at you because of that Garment Center contract?"

Beady eyes look up at him. "How you know about Garment Centers? Henny tell you?"

Coley blew smoke. "I got sharp ears. I heard Henny laced it into you the other day."

Rodriguez frowned. "One crazy guy. That Cantor tough. So Henny mad."

"Don't let him worry you so much."

Rodriguez gave a rueful grin. "Henny don't worry me. It's that Cantor. You don't know about that guy."

Coley shrugged. "I got ears."

Rodriguez's eyes and mouth became small and angry. "Dave Rodriguez soften him up, you wait and see. No more pussyfoot. Carlyle tell Henny that. Cantor gotta go, one way or the other, he got to listen."

Coley's insides tightened into a knot. "He's an old man."

What's it my business for, he thought, what's he to me?

Rodriguez dropped his dead cigar on the floor, stepped on it savagely. "I break down Cantor, I get five thousand dollar bonus. I got damn good plans." He gave Coley a quick look, then as if he'd spoken too much on the subject, he said. "How's your little boy?"

Coley fumbled for his cigarettes. "You get rough with Cantor and you're liable to raise a stink that'll blow this Syndicate wide open."

Rodriguez shrugged nonchalantly. "Don't worry your head about it, my friend."

"If you say so." His hands were wet and clammy and he couldn't understand it.

Butt out of it, Coley. Cantor's not your headache.

"Dave," Coley said abruptly. "How about me buying you a drink?"

Rodriguez ran a pink tongue over tobacco-flecked lips. "You my friend, Coley?"

Coley laughed. "In this business who's got friends?"

He slapped Coley's back. "You said it, *amigo*. You, Coley, you my friend 'cause I say so. I drink with you."

In a bar on Cherry Street they found seats in a corner booth and filled their glasses from a pinch-necked bottle of Scotch and drank. While Coley swallowed some club soda for a chaser, Rodriguez again filled his whiskey glass.

Coley said, "When you coming up to see my new apartment, Dave?"

"You move?"

Coley lifted his glass. "Second Avenue. Five rooms for Mom, the boy and me. Billy's nuts about his room, pictures all around the place, airplane models on every hunk of furniture. Mom doesn't like Second Avenue, away from the old neighborhood. I told her, she wants to visit, all she has to do is take a cab."

Rodriguez gulped down a drink. "I got nice place,

but my wife, she want to move uptown." He stared at the whiskey bottle as if it were a crystal ball. "I break Cantor, we move uptown."

"Don't bet on it."

"I got sure thing."

"Six feet of cemetery ground is the closest thing to a sure thing."

Rodriguez grinned. "I don't miss." He glanced around him then folded his arms on the table and leaned on them. "This is you and me talking, nobody else."

Coley found himself confused. "Maybe you should keep it to yourself."

Rodriguez said, "I break Cantor, I be big man in Syndicate. You ever hear of Duke Regan? He is big man in National Syndicate. He is Carlyle boss. He tell Carlyle, produce or get off the pot. You understand? Carlyle got to get Cantor for Duke Regan. So if I break Cantor I don't be big man in Syndicate?"

"I suppose so. But if you hurt Cantor and he goes to the cops?"

Rodriguez' eyes were glazed, as if covered by a film. "Cantor go no place. He be too scared. Listen, *amigo*, Cantor work late every Friday night. I check good. The Cantor woman goes to synagogue Friday night on Eastern Parkway. When it get real dark she come home. Cantor got no maid, no butler, no nothing. I got two friends in Detroit, they do anything for Dave Rodriguez and a couple bucks. I whistle and my boys grab next plane."

Coley watched Rodriguez fill his glass again, fling the liquid into his mouth, some of the whiskey dribbling down to his chin.

Rodriguez wiped it away with the back of his hand. "When Cantor woman come home from synagogue, my boys follow into house, tie her up good, dump her in bedroom. Soon Cantor come home. My boys tell him how his wife is someplace else and if he don't sign paper, he never see her again. Betcha life Cantor sign.”

Cold tension pulled at Coley's throat. “What's this paper, a sales agreement?”

“*Si*. Thirty per cent Cangro's for a song.” His lips looked swollen with slobber. “Carlyle wants twenty-five per cent, I get him thirty. I got good mouthpiece who draw up papers like I want and no questions.”

“Suppose Cantor doesn't sign?”

Rodriguez' eyes were dark smoldering agates. “I break his goddamn head, so help me.” He pounded the table and yelled for the bartender to bring another bottle of Scotch. “He will sign because Cantor do anything for his old lady.”

“You talked this over with anybody?”

“I don't need to; this is my job.”

“Carlyle won't like it, it's too damn risky.”

“I talk to nobody.”

“Henny ...”

“Nobody.” He look the bottle out of the bartender's hands. “Now no more talk.”

Coley's heart shook with pangs of conscience. “You can't just tie up that old lady like a bag of garbage. You'll hurt her. I just don't want you to get yourself and the Syndicate jammed up. It's a loco scheme, Dave. I'm your friend and I'm telling you forget it.”

Rodriguez stared. “Maybe I'm loco talking to you, Coley. You tell nobody about this, you hear me?”

Coley said, “Crazy as hell—”

Rodriguez cried, “I don't drink with you no more.” He pushed himself up, dropped bills on the table. “I pay for the whiskey. You tell one word to somebody ...” He left the threat dangling in the air. “*Adios*.”

Coley watched him go out of the bar on unsteady legs, then picked up the bottle and filled his glass.

This is Rodriguez' party, he thought, and there's nothing I can do about it. He drank quickly, trying to drown the turmoil going on inside him, and by the time he'd finished the bottle, succeeded.

Thursday Coley spent the entire day following a sidewalk whiskey salesman to his home, where the man filled pint bottles with a mixture of coloring extract and rotgut to be sold for thirty-five cents a bottle. Coley arrested the bootlegger, booked him at the precinct and lodged him in the Tombs for the night. In the morning the Alcoholic Beverage Control violation would be heard by the Magistrate. His assignment completed, Coley drove down to the Water Street warehouse where he found Dave Rodriguez pacing the office floor. The man looked tired, the area under his eyes was puffed and dark with shadows.

"I don't sleep so good," he explained. "I got things on my mind. That Cantor business ..."

Irritation in his tone, Coley said, "I thought you'd give up that crazy idea. Forget it, Dave. Tomorrow you and I'll go to the fights at the Garden. That Baker will knock hell out of your *amigo*, Pedro Garcia."

Rodriguez shrugged. "Who cares? I got plenty headache. You want a drink, Coley, my friend?"

"No, thanks."

Rodriguez took a bottle out of the desk, uncorked it, lifted it to his fat lips for a swallow.

The door opened and Henny Woods came into the room, stopping in his tracks as Rodriguez set down the bottle and wiped his mouth with the back of his large hairy hand.

"What the hell's the celebration?" Woods said savagely.

Rodriguez stiffened. "A little drink don't hurt."

"You it hurts plenty. You can't drink and keep your senses. Booze makes you soft in the head."

Rodriguez cried, "You don't talk to me like that."

Woods took a blunted cigar out of his mouth. "Gartoni got three months in the workhouse for making book. Gartoni should never have been arrested. You screwed that up good. You sent Gartoni to prison."

Rodriguez was indignant. "What you say, Henny? You crazy?"

"You should've iced the division cop."

"The cop don't take nothing."

"A hundred bucks and Gartoni'd never go to prison."

Rodriguez' cheeks were a smoldering red. "I try like anything. The cop don't listen."

Woods flung aside his cigar. "Now how does it look; we can't protect our member against a prison sentence?"

Rodriguez' morale was dissolving under Woods' relentless attack. "I say to cop, 'Here's hundred dollars on the floor. Pick it up.' The cop say, 'You don't get out of here, bud, I'll lock you up, too.' You ask Gartoni."

Woods gave him a strained sardonic look. "Gartoni says if you didn't have a load on you'd have taken the cop to one side to talk business. The cop was a probationary division man. He didn't dare take you up on your deal with Gartoni as a witness."

"False!" Rodriguez shouted. "This cop don't take ice."

"How can you be so dumb to try a bribe in front of witnesses?"

Rodriguez rubbed his face with his ten fingers. "I forget. It happens to anybody."

"Excuses," Woods said. "Stupid excuses. Dave, I hope to hell I can keep this from Carlyle."

Rodriguez sat down, cold and shaken. "No tell Carlyle."

Woods took a fresh cigar out of his coat pocket. "All right, Dave. I know you need this job and I want you to have it because you've been a good man. But I can't protect you forever." He lighted his cigar and said to Coley through the smoke screen. "There's another fifty in your envelope this pay day. You're doing a swell job. Keep it up."

Coley grinned. "Thanks, boss."

When Woods had gone, Rodriguez unburdened himself explosively. "You hear him, Coley, you hear?"

"I'm not deaf."

Something desperate grew in Rodriguez' expression. "I show him, I show him good."

Coley felt a vague apprehension. "Don't let him get you down."

"I get Cantor in my pocket. I be so big with Carlyle, I can spit on Woods. Then I be big dog, not Henny."

Coley shook his head. "You'll wind up in the can. Cantor will go to the police, even if you do get him to sign a paper, then you'll be up the creek, the Syndicate will be on the spot and the signed agreement would be worth toilet paper, only not so soft."

Rodriguez clenched his fists. "Cantor don't go to cops. My boys get him so scared that maybe they come back again to kill his wife, that Cantor will crap in his pants."

Coley cried, "Suppose he doesn't scare?"

Rodriguez laughed harshly. "So what do I lose? Nothing. I don't even go in that bum's house. My boys take care of everything while I be waiting down the street. Then my boys go back to Detroit. If Cantor hollers, who they gonna lock up? If he don't holler, Dave Rodriguez is top banana."

"A paper medal you'll get. Think it over for a couple weeks."

"Tomorrow I can't go to fights with you."

Coley stiffened. "Tomorrow? You got to plan this ..."

"It's planned good."

"You stupid jackass, can't you listen a minute?"

"What for you mad, Coley?"

"I'm not mad. Oh, what's the use of talking to you." Coley turned and ran out of the office.

Friday was a mild April afternoon.

Coley, Ben Fields and a sharp-eyed photographer sat in a police car with Lieutenant Breitel, waiting for the raid signal. Inspector Northern had ordered Coley and Ben Fields to assist five division men in a raid on the suspect premises of Philip Sanek, a wealthy man with residences in New York, Connecticut and Palm Beach. The nefarious activities of Sanek were no secret to the columnists. Once Walter Winchell had commented about a Saturday evening orgy in the Sanek residence, warning the man his affairs were under scrutiny by the police. A week later mention of another party was made by Ed Sullivan.

The columnists were right. Police had been working on the case.

Pursuant to an order of the Supreme Court authorizing the police "to listen to, intercept, overhear and make copies of telephone calls," a three-man detail had tapped Philip Sanek's New York telephone in an effort to get a lead on where and when the next party would be held. Twice the wire-tappers got word to the Commissioner, who immediately notified the Inspector in the divisional area where the party was scheduled. Each time the raided premises contained nothing but furniture.

This time, Inspector Northern was determined, the assignment would be successfully completed.

Lieutenant Breitel slipped gum between his big yellow teeth. "You want some, Walsh? Hey, Walsh, you with us or not?"

Coley, looking out the open car window, jumped. "You talking to me, sir?"

"That was my intention, but I'm better off talking to myself. Maybe I'd get an answer."

Coley said, "Sorry. My mind was miles away."

All night he'd been up, walking the floor, his conscience knotted with questions. He couldn't let the old man or the old lady get hurt, yet he couldn't buck Rodriguez and the Syndicate. ... Like a bundle of rags they'd tie her up, slap her around.

Coley stirred restlessly. "What's taking so long?"

Fields said. "It's five o'clock. Any minute now."

Minutes ticked by slowly.

Two division men were crouched outside the rear ground floor apartment on Sutton Place. One straightened, moved out of the alley to give the signal.

"Okay," Lieutenant Breitel said, "Let's go. Walsh, get the lead out, will you?"

They piled out of the car. While one took the doorman to one side to explain their mission, the others filed into the hallway to station themselves outside the apartment door.

The two men on the fire escape kicked in the window pane and jumped into the room.

"Stay put," they said, their badges displayed on their coat lapels, "and nobody will get hurt."

One opened the street door and Lieutenant Breitel and his men stalked into the apartment.

The police photographer ordered the three nude men and two nude girls, standing stunned in the center of the living room, not to move. Abruptly, one of the men, whom Coley recognized as Hilly Horton, a nephew of one of New York s biggest department store owners, made a break for the adjoining room.

"I want my clothes," he howled. "Somebody's gonna get in trouble for this."

One of the division men roughly pushed him back to the bare mattress in the center of the floor. "Try that again and I'll knock you on your ass."

A man sat in a chair, his arm around the blonde sitting on the chair arm. Philip Sanek and a red-haired girl sat on the mattress. Hilly Horton stood trembling as the photographer snapped two pictures.

Meanwhile, Coley and Ben Fields had inspected the premises and finding the kitchen door locked, pushed against it. A woman's frightened voice asked them to wait just a moment. Coley backed up, threw his weight on the door. It shook but held. Then the door was opened. A pretty girl, fully clothed down to the maid's apron and cap, came out blushing. Behind her a tall handsome man, also fully clothed, moved nonchalantly into the room. Coley blinked in amazement. The man was Winston Parker, one of Hollywood's best known actors, a man Coley had admired for his typically masculine roles. The maid's lipstick was smeared over her mouth. None showed on the man's face.

Fields said, "You making a picture in there, Mr. Parker?"

Parker's voice was strong, resonant, the kind of voice that had brought him thousands of fan letters every week.

"Is there anything wrong? The maid and I were just discussing my last picture, if that's a crime."

Coley said, "Get into the living room with the others. Maybe we could take a couple pictures of you and that gang in there. Your fans should like that."

Parker said easily, "May I use the phone?"

"Lieutenant Breitel is running this show. Ask him."

Permission was granted and within the half hour two lawyers and a representative of Winston Parker's motion picture studio appeared on the scene. By that time Inspector Northern had arrived to take full charge. The inspector and the lawyers huddled in a corner for a few minutes after which Parker was permitted to leave, free of all charges.

Fields said, "It's just as well. The notoriety would probably triple his fan mail. People are like that. Anyway, we got no case against him. He wasn't in the room with the others and we caught him with his pants on. Petting isn't a crime. We could pinch him on a disorderly conduct but he'd beat the case and it'd do him more good than us."

Coley said, "I guess you're right."

He went to the window, looked out at the sun fading from view behind an apartment house. Soon dusk would close in on the city. Then it would get dark and it would be the beginning of the Sabbath, time for Mrs. Cantor to come home from the synagogue ...

He felt suddenly weak and limp as if his muscles and bones were turning to putty.

Inspector Northern eyed him sharply. "Walsh, you look like a sick dog. The sight of those bums make me sick too, but ..."

Cold resolve clasped tightly around his throat. "I don't feel well. It's my head and stomach, some kind of virus. Could I be excused?"

The blonde was answering the lieutenant's questions. "I'm eighteen. I'm a model. No, I don't get paid for this. It's just that a girl meets the right kind of people, guys who can help her career."

Inspector Northern sighed. "We got enough men to carry on without you. You're excused, Walsh."

Coley drove to the warehouse on Water Street. Henny Woods would have to stop Rodriguez. He just had to. Woods or Carlyle, one of them would listen to common sense ...

## Eleven

It was six-thirty-five when Coley walked into the warehouse so busy with his thoughts he failed to give his customary greeting to the men working around the table. Henny Woods, leaning over a ledger on his office desk, jumped to attention when Coley slammed the door closed.

"Take it easy," Woods said.

"Henny, you gotta stop Dave before he hurts that Cantor woman."

Woods grunted. "What you talking about?"

Quickly Coley told the story of Rodriguez'

ambitious program for that evening and when he'd finished, Woods seemed to have found something amusing in what he said.

Coley cried, "This is no joke. This could mean the Syndicate."

Woods waved his hand. "Don't be a fool. This Syndicate is too strong these days to worry about a guy like Cantor."

"Don't be so overconfident. Carlyle should get an earful of this crazy plan."

Woods' eyes narrowed. "What's all this to you?"

"I know Cantor. I know the old lady. I don't want to sit on my hands while some damn Detroit hoods bang them around."

Henny's eyebrows lifted. "So you know Cantor?"

"Carlyle knows him too. Make something of that. Look, Henny, I got no time to explain to you right now. By seven-fifteen or seven-thirty the old lady will be coming home. You and I got to be there to see nobody bothers her."

Woods scowled. "It's Dave's party. And you know something? I think it's got a good chance to work. In any case that Cantor will know we're tired of fooling around."

Coley's muscles tightened. "You tell Carlyle the score or I will. He knows Cantor—"

"You said that, and let me tell you something, Carlyle wouldn't waste spit on the old bastard. He hates Cantor's guts. That weasel is holding up Pete's big project and Pete ain't taking any more crap. For his own protection—after all, his boss, Duke Regan, wants results—he's got to step on Cantor good."

"Damn you, call Carlyle—"

"Carlyle's out of town. He'll be back tomorrow. You and me, Coley'll tell him the whole story. Satisfied?"

"You won't help me stop Rodriguez?"

Woods pointed his finger. "Butt out, cop."

Coley spat two words at him, wheeled around and left the room.

Nervous tension pulled at Coley's stomach as he stopped his car a block before Cantor's house. It was late, and Coley had no doubt that Mrs. Cantor had come home. How was she at the moment? Had they hurt her? Somehow, he would help the Cantors and somehow, it would be a clean operation, no rough stuff, no shooting, nothing that would bring in the police and their investigations.

If only he could find Dave Rodriguez!

Out of the car, he walked up the street, his eyes searching every alley, every stoop, every hallway. Rodriguez could stop his men. Had Dave gone inside the house? He'd said he'd not endanger his safety by showing his face.

"Dave!"

Leaning idly against a pump, Rodriguez turned his head, stared blankly.

Coley said, "If your boys are in that house, get 'em out."

Rodriguez' eyes gleamed in the semi-darkness. "My boys inside and they get out when the job is finished."

"Dave," Coley pleaded, "get your boys out or I'll do it for you."

"Wait one minute," Rodriguez growled. When people stopped to stare, Rodriguez whirled on them. "What you want?" Quickly, they walked on. Rodriguez said to Coley, "Butt in and I kill you like a dog, Coley. You hear? I work too hard to stop now." He stared over Coley's head. "Now comes that Cantor."

Joseph Cantor, his short squat body silhouetted by the corner street light, turned into his driveway. Coley cried out. A startled woman stopped, her mouth open, but Cantor heard nothing.

Rodriguez grasped Coley's arm. "You listen to me,

you son of a—"

Coley hooked his left hand into Rodriguez' tremendous belly, brought his right hand down on the man's neck. Coley leaped over the man sprawled in the gutter, raced across the street, hopped over the hedges.

Coley saw Cantor open the door. The foyer lights flickered on just before the door closed. Coley raced up the paved walk. He heard a shout, shrill with fear, as he pushed open the door. Running toward Coley, his lips working but nothing coming out, Cantor held his arms out like a child asking to be helped. Behind Cantor a bull-headed man moved in giant strides, a black revolver held in his right fist.

"Coley!" Cantor managed to cry out. "Please, Coley." The gun landed with a sickening thud, and Cantor sprawled at Coley's feet.

Coley cried out, "Dave sent me to tell you guys to blow."

The man didn't hear or didn't care. Momentum had carried him forward. He lifted his gun and as it came down, Coley ducked under and away, slammed his fist into the man's face. The man reeled drunkenly. Coley hit him again and the man stretched out on the floor.

The shot sounded loud in the tense quiet. Startled, Coley turned, dropped to one knee. The second man, short and thin, stood straddle-legged in the semi-darkness of the living room. Mouth open, breathing heavily, the man moved forward, waiting to get off another shot. Coley shouted Rodriguez' name. The man's gun jumped again and again, the sound of gunfire rolling around the room like thunder.

Swearing, Coley yanked out his .38 snub-nose. The man's fourth shot and Coley's first sounded as one, both missing. Coley pumped twice more. The man's lips opened wider, his gun dropping out of his hand. His left eye spurting blood, he went down, first his knees then the rest of him sprawled in a grotesque heap.

Coley felt a tight thrill, a calmness like steel as he went into the living room and looked down at the man. He heard a movement at the door, turned in time to see the big man run out of the house. Coley made no move to go after him. There would be enough to explain now.

Groaning, Cantor stirred, rolled, lunged drunkenly to his feet. "Bessie," he cried. "What they done to my Bessie?"

Coley shoved his revolver into its holster, tried the bedroom door. Cantor, a step behind him, flicked on the lights. Mrs. Cantor lay face up on the bed, her arms under her, a wide strip of adhesive spread across her mouth. Her breath came out in a rasp and there was a bluish tinge in her cheeks.

Cantor cried, "The *Shabbas* candles I don't see lit, I know something is wrong."

Coley pushed Cantor away, ripped off the adhesive in one quick motion, turned her sideways on the bed to rip off the adhesive which held her wrists together.

In a hoarse voice barely louder than a whisper, Cantor begged, "Speak to me, Bessie, please, God."

Slowly her eyes opened and she clutched her chest. "I got such a pain. Yussel, such a terrible pain."

Coley cried, "Get a doctor, quick."

Cantor stared, completely stunned.

The door opened and a wide-eyed policeman came into the room, his revolver in his hand.

Coley showed his badge. "Get a doctor, quick. Heart attack."

Puffing on a cigarette, Coley sat on a straight-backed chair in the large kitchen, his gaze following Inspector Storey as he came away from the assistant district attorney. Joseph Cantor sat at the kitchen table, hands tensely clasped in his lap. Mille stood behind him, her eyes full of tears. Coley looked up, gave her a reassuring wink. The stenographer conferred with Assistant District Attorney Feldman, a freckle-faced man wearing large horn-rimmed glasses.

The sound of movement, talking, flash bulbs popping, drifted into the kitchen.

The assistant district attorney said, "As we understand it, Walsh, you came visiting your girl friend, Miss Raft, saw Mr. Cantor entering his house and decided to say hello. You reached the front lawn and heard a moan or a scream, and ran inside the house just in time to see Mr. Cantor slugged by this big man."

Coley said, "That's right. It was quite dark and I didn't get a look at Mr. Cantor's assailant."

The assistant district attorney said, "The second man took a shot at you but you got him first." He looked at the inspector for confirmation. "That wraps up Walsh's story."

The inspector nodded. "A good thing Walsh came visiting Miss Raft. No telling what those men might have done."

Joseph Cantor said fervently, "Thank God. Not for Coley, the murderers kill us away like nothing."

Coley said, "I don't believe they were out to kill anybody, unless somebody got in their way. This was a simple case of attempted robbery."

Feldman said, "That isn't what Mr. Cantor suggested."

Cantor looked apologetic. "Could be I was wrong."

Feldman said, "Mr. Cantor suggests that this might have been an attempt to coerce him into selling a piece of his business to a crooked syndicate."

Coley smiled. "I don't believe it. This syndicate, whoever they are, can't be composed of morons. These tactics wouldn't work with Mr. Cantor. I know the man. The moment those men left he'd go running to the nearest police station. Those men were out to burglarize this house."

Inspector Storey said, "I'll buy the robbery and burglary theory. Walsh did a fine job. The department is proud of him."

Cantor said, "I am proud too."

Coley said, "Why don't you go see how the missus is?"

Cantor rose unsteadily to his feet. "Maybe now they let me talk to my Bessie."

It was ten o'clock when the doctor finally came out of Mrs. Cantor's room. Mille and Coley sat side by side on the couch, their eyes following Cantor as he got up and walked haltingly up to the handsome man with the bronzed features.

Cantor raised his hands in a plea. "Dr. Linett ..."

Dr. Linett's smile radiated confidence. "Mrs. Cantor is resting comfortably now. I will return in the morning. The nurse knows what to do and where to reach me if necessary."

Joseph Cantor's eyes were dry and feverish. "Don't let her die, Doctor."

Dr. Linett, lean and stiff-jointed, walked to the doorway. "We won't. The electrocardiograph shows some damage to the heart, but it could have been a lot worse."

Cantor said feelingly, pointing to Coley. "Not for Coley, my Bessie dies tied up like a dog. Coley, you I owe my life, and my Bessie's life, too."

Coley said, "The hell with that."

Dr. Linett's sharp gray eyes swept Coley's face. "After five or six weeks at home, we'll pack Mrs. Cantor off to Florida for a couple of months and she'll come home a brand new woman. Good night."

Cantor walked the doctor to the door and in a few moments returned to the living room. "It's a terrible feeling," he said, staring into space. "Like I'm alone in the world."

Mille said, "You better not let Mrs. Cantor hear you say that."

Cantor's voice had a hollow ring. "Nobody to talk a word to." He smiled faintly. "Nobody to holler on."

Mille said, "Holler at me if it'll make you feel better."

Cantor gave her a grateful look. "Yes, my Mille, you I still got and Coley, son."

Coley said, "Never thought I'd get to be a millionaire's son."

"Coley, if there's something ..."

Coley laughed. "You can lend me ten bucks."

Repentant, Cantor looked away. "You know why I didn't lend you that money you once asked me for? Because Joseph Cantor is an old fool. Too much business in the head. Thousands I give every year to charity. To you I say no. I'm not an old fool?"

Coley said, "Forget it, Pop."

Cantor's eyes lit up with an idea. "Coley, I got a proposition like you never heard before. My own son I couldn't give a better proposition."

Coley lighted a cigarette, said nothing.

"Come in business with me," Cantor beamed. "No more police. I got nobody except my Bessie, Mille, you. Coley, I learn you the trade A to Z. When I die you and my Bessie will be partners. Then my Bessie will make a living and you and Mille will make a living. In my pine box I will be a happy man. Well, Coley?"

Coley picked up the ash tray, laid it down. "I'm doing all right, Pop."

Cantor hung his head, as if he'd been humiliated. "You got a chance to be a partner in a business what's been established. You get security."

"That's not security. Things can happen to jobs. New bosses can make nothing out of the best job in the world."

Cantor's eyes were filled with unshed tears. "All my life I will remember what I done and what you done tonight for me and my Bessie. Coley, listen to me. What good is the business if I can't leave it to somebody, a son or a daughter? I gonna give you fifteen per cent; fifteen shares of Cangro's, and when you come into the business, Coley, my boy, I give you ten shares more."

His lips suddenly dry, Coley stared at him.

Mille threw her arms around him. "Coley, this is wonderful."

Pangs of regret shook his heart. He could have saved Mrs. Cantor, if he hadn't waited, if he had stopped Rodriguez the first time the Puerto Rican had spilled his guts about how he would break Cantor.

Gently he pushed Mille away. "Pop, you're talking from heat."

Cantor said, "Monday, my lawyer will have the papers ready. Coley, look a little happy."

Coley cried, "What is there to be happy about? Your wife's in there maybe dying ..."

And I could have saved her!

Mille looked worried. "Coley, where are you going?"

He stared at his hand on the doorknob. "For a walk or something. I don't know."

She said, "I'll go with you."

"I want to walk alone."

Cantor said, "Don't forget, Monday ..."

Coley shouted. "Cut it out, will you, for God's sake, leave me alone."

He yanked at the door and closed it behind him.

## Twelve

The Walsh's five-room apartment, overlooking a small park on Second Avenue, had been furnished by Mrs. Walsh with money given her by Coley. To Coley the furnishings were beautiful even though for some reason he couldn't understand, the red drapes didn't seem to blend in with the persimmon frieze-covered living-room set. The red-painted bedroom walls didn't exactly clash with the forest green drapes and bed covering, yet somehow they didn't look quite right. The dark blue kitchen was small but there was enough room in the dinette for a mahogany table and four matching chairs.

In his shirt sleeves, Coley sat in the living room, watching Billy work his way on crutches across the floor, his left leg in a brace, moving stiffly.

Coley said, "Attaboy, Bill, you sure surprised me."

Triumph shining in his soft brown eyes, Billy said, "Molly the nurse said I'll be playing baseball real soon. Will I, Dad, huh, will I?"

Coley took him in his arms, the crutches dropping. "You betcha life. Tomorrow, when you go back to the hospital, you keep trying twice as hard."

The boy's face fell. "I have to go back, Dad?"

"You have to, boy. Next time maybe they'll let you come home for a whole week. How'll that be?"

Tears were in the boy's eyes. "Okay, I guess. Only you hardly come see me in the hospital."

Coley felt guilty. "I've been so busy, but I'll be up Wednesday, cross my heart. Now you got to rest. You want me to carry you into your bedroom?"

The boy shook his head. "Nah. I can make it easy."

He helped the boy get set with the crutches, then watched Billy work his way across the room. Mom, coming in from the kitchen, followed the boy to his bedroom.

The telephone rang twice, then was quiet.

"Coley," Mom called, "it's Mille. She sounds worried."

Coley took the receiver out of her hand. "Yeh, Mille?"

"Mr. Cantor's been hurt."

"What happened?"

"Hit-and-run driver."

"Hurt bad?"

"Thank God, no. A lot of bruises and scratches. It's mostly shock. He's in bed now. I can hear him now yelling for the doctor to go treat his horse patients."

Coley said, "Was it an accident, the hit-and-run, I mean?"

"I don't know, Coley. He says the car missed him by inches. First it was coming right at him, then abruptly swerved. Coley, come out. I want you here. I feel so lonely ..."

"See you in twenty minutes."

A woolen robe wrapped snugly around him, Joseph Cantor was sitting on the couch when Coley came into the house.

With gestures, Cantor explained. "If my Bessie knows I'm in bed she'll come out to tend me like I was sick." There were hollows under his eyes and the darkness of worry was in his face. "I don't know what's going to be with her."

Mille said, "I'll tell you what's going to be with her. In six weeks Mrs. Cantor will go to Florida and you'll keep her company."

Cantor was very depressed. "In six weeks we could be dead and buried. Coley, you didn't come to my office like I asked."

Coley took out a cigarette, studied the brand name. "My boss kept me busy handing out two-buck summonses."

Cantor took an envelope lying on the table, slipped out a sheaf of legal paper.

"A lot of words," he said. "But all in all you're a junior partner, fifteen per cent worth, my boy. Here sign the contract."

Coley made no move. "You sure were in a hurry, Pop."

"What's to wait? Who knows what can be tomorrow? Only Friday I had a healthy wife. Today she's sick. This morning I was strong like a ox. Tonight I got a pain in my belly. I'm frightened, Coley, for the first time in my life ... Next time they'll run me over like a bag of garbage."

"It was an accident," Coley said without conviction.

Cantor's lips twisted into a bitter smile. "Just before you came in, I got a telephone call."

Mille said, "They said next time the car would crawl up his back. Today was just a warning, his last one. The man spoke so loudly I could hear him from where I stood near Mr. Cantor."

"See?" Cantor cried. "I don't lie to you. For me, I don't care so much ..."

"We got to fight them, Pop."

"But my Bessie, I'm afraid for my wife."

Coley got up, took a half turn around the room, the mounting anger burning inside him. "We'll get her protection. Pop, you can't lay down now; they'll walk all over you."

Mille said, "Would the police help?"

Coley blew air into his fist. "Police protection, that's all they can give him now. He's got no case against anybody. A cop'd never make a collar on the kind of evidence Pop can supply."

She looked him in the eye. "Maybe there are things you know ... real proof ...?"

"What are you talking about?"

"I just thought, you're a cop, Coley. Maybe there are things you've heard, facts you know that could be tied up with whoever it is that's after Mr. Cantor."

"I don't know anything that could help the situation."

"You don't know who is in back of this Syndicate?"

"A guy by the name of Duke Regan, who is one-third boss of a national syndicate. Not only don't I know who he is but there are probably very few people who do."

She stared at him, eyes bright and shiny. "I thought you'd name somebody nearer to home. I guess I was wrong."

He turned his back on her. "Well, Pop, you want to ask for police protection?"

Cantor was appalled. "What am I, a baby? A policeman walking beside me, day and night, inside, outside my house, so all the neighbors will think God knows what that Cantor did that a policeman got to watch him so he don't run away. Who needs it? For my Bessie I got a nurse. When Bessie starts to go out for little walks, in a month or so, I hire me a private detective."

"If that's how you want it," Coley said, "That's how it'll be. I'll say so long now. I got to see a guy."

Cantor held out the contract. "Sign both copies."

"Not tonight, Pop. When I'm in the mood, I'll grab the deal, believe me. Mille, walk me to the door? 'Bye, Pop."

She opened the door for him, kissed his lips. "Be careful, Coley. You don't have to look so surprised. I know exactly where you're going. Your chin is sticking out for somebody to bust it."

He laughed. "Keep guessing."

"Peter Carlyle is the head of the New York Syndicate, isn't he?"

"So long, baby ..."


The electric bulbs encased in wrought-iron cast subdued yellow light into Coley's face as he got out of his car and stood before Carlyle's gray stone house on East Sixty-fifth Street. The butler answered Coley's ring, Woods one step behind him.

In a voice as cold as his face, Woods said, "You got your nerve."

"I didn't come to see you." Coley pushed by the stocky man. "I want to talk to Pete. I understand he got home this morning."

"Pete doesn't need company, not a lousy double-crossing cop. You couldn't stay out of Rodriguez' business? You had to go out and make big black headlines?"

Not answering him, Coley walked into the living room. He had the feeling he'd stepped into a world he'd seen only in the moving pictures. He gaped at the luxurious brocade drapes, the pendant chandelier, the mahogany paneling on the walls, and the thick fawn-colored carpeting. The magnificence of the marble staircase with its gently curving balustrade stopped him in his tracks.

Woods' voice grated on his nerves. "You buying this house?"

"Maybe," Coley said softly. "You never can tell."

Coley wished Mille were here so she could enjoy the sight with him. She would love the tapestry that looked beautiful enough to have come from the Gobelins works in Paris. At least they looked like the pictures he'd seen.

Coley heard a grunt and turned just as Carlyle was coming down the last two steps of the staircase, his silk robe open at the knees. There was no rancor in the man's eyes, nor was there a sign of welcome.

Coley said, "I want a couple words with you, Pete."

Woods said, "On your knees, Walsh, and you'll still wind up in the gutter."

Carlyle went to a tapestry-covered chair, sat down. "Make it brief, Coley, I've got a date with my barber in fifteen minutes."

The butler, thin and gaunt, came in and mixed drinks to order. While Carlyle chewed on a big black cigar, Coley lighted a cigarette.

"Five minutes," Carlyle said brusquely. "I owe you that much."

Woods spat the words. "You owe him nothing, Pete. He had no business screwing up Rodriguez."

Coley said contemptuously, "I save your skin, yours and the Syndicate's. I snipped the fuse that could have blistered your big fat ass."

Woods snapped. "You're talking through a hole in your head."

Coley said to Carlyle, "Would you have permitted Rodriguez to go ahead with that crazy scheme to use Cantor's wife to blackjack Cantor?"

Carlyle blew smoke. "Coley, you should have minded your own business. Henny is your boss. You take orders from him. Oh, I know how your heart bled for that old man, but my heart stopped bleeding for people a long time ago, ever since my old man died in the gutter because he'd sold an extra pint of his blood for five badly needed dollars. Dave had no business telling you about Cangro's nor what he had planned."

Coley could feel the wall Carlyle was building between them. A little higher and he would never be able to scale it.

Coley said, "You didn't answer my question, Pete. Maybe what is good for this Syndicate isn't my business. Just answer me, would you have stopped Dave?"

Carlyle's level gaze didn't waver. "If one of those Detroit boys had been caught, there might have been hell to pay. It was a dangerous gamble. I like to play it safe. Harass, threaten, cajole, hit and duck away. Then they can't point the finger at you. In the old days we could mangle a guy's courage so that he was too frightened to go to the police. No reason why it shouldn't work today. But I prefer it the more subtle way. Besides, Cantor isn't an ordinary man. Even in the old days a guy like Cantor would have taken a beating and crawled to the police, on his hands and knees if he had to. But we'll soften him up, little by little ... until he either comes begging or winds up in a nuthouse."

Woods said, "Amen."

The atmosphere was thick with menace and cold cruelty.

Coley's voice was clear, almost triumphant. "That old man's got more guts than your whole pack of dogs, Pete. He'll beat you, and you'll wish you'd never started with him."

Carlyle's lips twitched. "Maybe I wish that now, Coley. But I did start and I must finish and he's got to be slugged into submission, one way or another. Next time maybe I'll give the signal to really give him a workout." He appraised Coley closely. "What do you think of that, Coley?"

"Better yet, I wonder what Cantor would think if he knew you were behind all his troubles. He once called you a gentleman with a high hat."

Carlyle said with genuine regret, "The Cantors are nice people. The few times I've spoken to them they were so hospitable I wished I could chuck the whole business."

"Why don't you?"

Carlyle heaved forward in his chair. There was fire in his gray eyes. "I've got no choice. It's him or me. He's a damn bottleneck I got to smash to get to a lot of other manufacturers. I got to break Cantor and I will."

"Suppose you don't break Cantor?"

"Then I'll resign my job."

"You mean you'll get fired, don't you?"

Carlyle looked blank. "You talk too much, Coley. Shut your damn hole!"

"For now, yes. But if anything happens to Cantor, you'll hear from me."

Woods cried, "What's it to you? Buttin' in ..."

Carlyle got up to stand in a crouch, one hand clutching a cigar, the other clenched at his side. "You said enough, Coley. For a two-buck cop, you got a damn nerve. Like Benny said, 'What's it to you?'"

Coley said, "Fifteen per cent of Cangro's. Cantor

has a contract all drawn. All I got to do is sign it. I will, soon as I earn that fifteen per cent."

Suspicion etched in every line of his scowling face, Carlyle said, "How did you ...? That business of saving Cantor's life, that's it, isn't it?"

Coley nodded. "Fifteen per cent, Pete. Ten more when I join the firm."

Carlyle clasped his head with both hands, the cigar falling out of his hand. "We break our hump to get a piece of Cangro's and you ...! Coley, I just thought of something."

Coley said easily, "I understand all such contracts protect the owner so that I can't sell any shares without offering them to him first, and only with his permission."

Carlyle waved his hand. "That's elementary. But once you're in, you're in a good position to convince Cantor it's for his best interests to take another partner. All the trouble he's having could be cleared up by a guy you know and recommend; a guy who has connections and could make these hoodlums toe the mark."

Coley said, "I should recommend you?"

Woods, cool and dangerous, said, "A little respect for the boss."

Carlyle's tone was conciliatory. "Coley, do you think you could have got into this Syndicate without my say-so? You don't really think you bluffed us into hiring you. That business of pushing our bookies around was strictly minor-league stuff. The boys wanted to shut you up for good. I stopped them."

"Thanks."

"I got you your job. You were a tough man, a guy with a badge I could use. And I liked you. So you were in."

"I produced for you."

"Naturally. But you should be a little grateful to me."

Coley gave a rueful, comprehending grin. "You made your point, and it's not strong enough."

"If you swing this deal, there's a package of big bills in it for you."

Coley lighted a cigarette, said nothing.

Carlyle picked up his cigar, dropped it into the ash tray, searched in the cigar box for another.

"Coley, anything less than thirty-five grand you pay for twenty-five shares, is yours. Fair enough?"

Coley said, "It's a lot of money."

"And," Carlyle said, "you'd always have a place in this Syndicate. Coley, I know about your son, Billy. This would be your big chance to really do something for him."

Coley killed his cigarette in the tray. "That's one of the reasons I got into the racket, that and a hungry feeling for the good old dollar. At least that's what I tell myself when I feel my cold conscience kicking up. One of those reasons is shot. I know my kid will never be any better."

"God has spoken," Carlyle said mockingly.

"Even the doctor doesn't kid me anymore. Sure Billy can use the massages and treatments but he doesn't need an expensive hospital and private nurses."

Carlyle said, "Let's not forget that good old dollar you mentioned."

Coley nodded, laughed. "I like my new apartment. I like my sharp clothes. I like to have an extra buck in my pocket so I don't have to figure pennies when a bum asks me for a quarter. Pete, it's nice."

Carlyle chuckled. "I know how you feel. Coley, you got that security in this organization. I got plans, a lot of plans, and they include you. How'd you like to quit the police and come in with us full time?"

Coley shook his head sadly. "It wasn't so long ago I had to beg for a forty-buck-a-week job. All of a sudden I got two big jobs."

"Then it's settled."

Coley held up his hand. "It is, like hell. That full time job you're giving me, it's to work on Cantor, isn't it?"

Carlyle looked surprised. "Of course. I'm paying you a salary to brainwash that old bastard—"

"It's no good, Pete. I couldn't do it. I don't want to do it."

Carlyle gave Coley a long glance. "I don't think I like your attitude, Coley."

"Lay off the old man and I'll come into the Syndicate full time."

All attempts of diplomacy gone, Carlyle cried, "Who the hell needs you?"

Coley got up. "It figures. Actually, I had a feeling our talk would end this way. I really came over to tell you to lay off the old man and go muscle somebody else."

"I'm laughing."

"I don't want to see the old man pushed around."

"I don't like your threats, expressed or implied."

The room suddenly became alien and hostile. "Lay off him, Pete."

Woods' eyes shone with malicious delight. "He's out, Pete, Coley's out of my hair."

Carlyle's face was white with anger. "Out on his ear! You know where you'll wind up, Coley? Behind a garbage can with the rest of the bums. Those fifteen shares won't be worth a dime once we take over Cangro's. Maybe I won't have to wait that long; start anything and if I have to, you'll take a trip in a concrete box to the bottom of the ocean. I'm not kidding, Coley."

Determination revealed itself in the rigid clamp of his lips. "If that's how it's got to be, Pete, I'll take a chance that you instead of me winds up in that box."

Woods cried, "Pete, you gonna let him just walk out. He knows too much."

Carlyle shook his head. "He knows nothing that won't get him jammed up if he opens his mouth. Let him go ..."

Coley went out, the butler appearing out of nowhere to hold open the door for him. Outside, he stood on the sidewalk and lit a cigarette, wondering if he should see a psychiatrist. Maybe the doctor could tell Coley Walsh why he felt such a gratifying sense of exhilaration giving up a big package of Syndicate money every week.

## Thirteen

The meeting was held in Cantor's reception room.

At Coley's insistence, Cantor had called together a dozen of the major dress manufacturers in the city. Six had shown up, another had sent a representative. Seated informally around the room, some smoked, some drank their favorite liquor, some found pleasure in doing both, alternately or together, or so it seemed to Coley. The noise of their talk and laughter was a pleasant drone of sound.

Simon Weiner, a short, chunky man with restless gray eyes, slapped the table. "Gentlemen, please, we gonna sit and shmooze all night? Let's get this nonsense over with."

Joseph Cantor, who had, been whispering with Coley, looked up, startled. "Nonsense? This you call nonsense, Mr. Weiner? There is trouble in the whole Garment Center. Don't you know that?"

Weiner was brisk and incisive. "There's always trouble. We gonna clean it up? What are we, magicians? I can't talk for every rag manufacturer here, but for Elite Originals, I can say the little troubles we got is all personal and we can handle it. I bet so can my other friends here. What we're doing here, I don't understand."

Cantor said as if explaining to a wayward child,

"We got to keep racketeers and bloodsuckers from the Syndicate out of Seventh Avenue."

"Racketeers? Syndicate?" Weiner cried in shocked amazement. "Don't exaggerate so much, Cantor, please. A couple troublemakers, ten-cent shakedown artists, yes, but they're lone wolves we can slap down."

Dave Simpson, lean, stiff-jointed, his mouth tight under the small mustache, stood up. "Simon, stop with the laughing. This is not funny. I got trouble too and it's not with a ten-cent hoodlum."

Weiner waved his hand. "Everybody's got trouble. My secretary ran off with my accountant, a married man, so I know what trouble is because today a good secretary don't grow on trees. Business thrives on trouble. But to talk about organized racketeers is ridiculous. Right, Abe?"

Abe Gross, of Gross and Nussbaum, Inc., said emotionlessly, "Ridiculous."

Coley rose to his feet. "Perhaps I could say a word."

Weiner's thick eyebrows lifted. "Who are you, may I ask?"

"Coley Walsh. Mr. Cantor introduced us."

"I didn't mean that. Who is Coley Wash? That part I didn't get when Joseph introduced us."

Cantor said, "Coley is interested in our troubles."

"I still don't know who he is."

Dark eyes shining with anger, Coley said, "I'll write you a book. I'm a junior member of Cangro's. Or at least I will be some day. I got a future in Cangro's I want to protect."

Weiner, unperturbed at Coley's temper, said, "You still got no standing here, my good friend."

"Let him talk," Simpson said. "What is this, a Soviet election, a man can't open his mouth?"

Shrugging his powerful shoulders, Weiner, a look of boredom on his cherubic face, leaned back in his chair.

Coley looked around him. "Yesterday, in the Federal Building on Foley Square, I had a fifteen-minute talk with the Counsel of the Senate rackets investigating committee. The Senate committee, as you all know, is now investigating labor unions. Meanwhile, they are gathering evidence on rackets in industry. The counsel for the committee, Senator Kennedy, has promised a full investigation of the Garment Center. What evidence the Senator has compiled I wouldn't know but what I do know is that the Senator would like the manufacturers to help him drive the hoods out of the Center by giving him facts and figures."

"Just a minute," Weiner jumped up. Outrage ringing in his every word, he cried, "You telling me that you, a nobody in the dress business, presumed to represent us in a talk with the Committee Counsel?"

In Coley's tone was a faint suggestion of mockery. "What are you so frightened about, Mr. Weiner? I represented nobody but myself, a private citizen interested in a clean Center."

"Who asked you?" Bright red blotches spread over his ample face. "As far as we are concerned there is no racketeering, as you call it, in our business."

Simpson said, "Where do you get that 'we' stuff?"

Werner's head came around in a short, stiff turn. "You got trouble with racketeers?"

"I got trouble."

"You can prove that to a Senate committee?"

"I don't know what legal proof is in a courtroom. Anyway, even if what I know is good evidence, I can't talk about it." His eyes mirrored his anguish. "Frankly, I'm afraid to talk."

Coley said, "If you people stick together you can put fear into those goons."

Joseph Cantor's voice trembled. "Only then can we retain our self-respect, our dignity. When we were younger we had troubles with goons, in the twenties, remember? We beat them because, after years of paying tribute, we decided to hell with those bloodsuckers and we fought them like they was a black plague. We'll fight them and beat them again."

Rocco Lazetta of Rolla Creations, Inc., a tall man whose clothes hung loosely on his thin-boned frame, waved his hand and shouted, "Maybe some of us got real proof, first class information, that could really give those bastards the business." His lips became slack, his face tormented. "But I got a wife and children. Rolla Creations and all the profits in the world couldn't pay for their lives."

Cantor pleaded, "Integrity, pride, they mean nothing? Rocco, my friend, I got a wife too. And you don't think I am frightened? But I got to live with myself, and in the morning when I shave, that face I see in the mirror, I don't want it should make me sick. Fight the plague, kill it before it kills us."

Weiner said quietly, "What if we die with it?"

Bob Brown, representing Pedigree Originals, shifted his big body to a more comfortable position. "At least we die on our feet."

Weiner bowed in a mocking way. "For that you'll get a tin medal which they'll bury with you. Some of us want to live, we want our families to live in peace."

Cantor cried, "A minute ago you wouldn't admit we got racketeers in the Center."

Weiner sighed. "It's smarter sometimes to do like the monkey, who puts his hands over his eyes."

Coley said, somewhat impatiently, "The Senator knew what he was talking about. His greatest difficulty, he said, was in getting cooperation from the people who needed help the most. Fear, self-interest, makes people reluctant to talk."

Weiner moved out of his chair, steely authority in his manner. "You got a lot of nerve, Walsh. If this was my office I'd ask you to get the hell out of here. Who the hell died and made you my boss? I've been in the rag business since before you were born. I fear nobody and nothing. Self-interest? Yes, but not the way you mean it. I don't like the reputation of this industry torn down by somebody sticking his nose into things that don't concern him. The public has respect for the manufacturers in the dress business. And they should because we are respectable, reputable men. Now you come along and try to tear down our reputation. All of a sudden you decide we are holding hands with racketeers. You think the Senate investigation will be a wonderful thing for this business? You're wrong. Because after it's all over, after the investigation, the big speeches and the hearings, some poor heel will get two months in jail for perjury, and the big shots will be free and loose and tougher than ever, and we in the business will have a big black eye."

Breathing heavily, Weiner slumped down in his seat. For a minute it was quiet, then Matt Dennis of Teenage Dress Company, an elderly man wearing big horn-rimmed glasses, raised his dry, thin voice.

"Simon Weiner is worried about our reputation. So am I. Not that I don't see no evil. God knows there's plenty of dirt. And we gotta sweep it out before the investigation committee throws the spotlight on us." He took a deep breath as if talking was sapping his strength. "Somebody shoulda come here a year ago and told me what's going on. Then maybe I'da had sense enough not to take a partner just because he offered me a fancy price for thirty per cent of Teenage. I'd like to tell that committee what's happened to my business since I got me a partner."

Weiner interrupted. "Maybe the Senator will think you're just trying to get rid of a partner. It's possible."

Dennis stood staring down at Weiner, anger rippling behind the surface of his dark eyes. "If you could see the trouble I got since my partner came into the firm. Trouble in the shop, trouble in the shipping department, even the size tags can't seem to stay on the garments."

Weiner said, "You can prove it's your partner's fault?"

"No," Dennis said, "But it figures. Since—"

"Proof," Weiner cried. "That's what the committee will need. I got troubles with my wife, she should break a leg, and I'd like to get rid of her, but the committee won't help me. You sold a piece of your business and now you'd like to get it back, a present from this God-Almighty committee?"

Dennis sat down. "I can't argue with you, Weiner. I get tired so easy these days."

"You're a damn fool," Weiner cried. "One foot in the grave and you're worried maybe your partner isn't carrying on the business in your old-fashioned ways. Before you die maybe you can make arrangements to take the business with you. Cheating, everybody cheating, but you."

Simpson yelled, "You should know about that, Weiner."

Coley stood helplessly calling for order, nobody paying attention. Among these men there was a bit of antagonism, animosity, resentment; there were too many jarring personalities.

Coley cried out something obscene and as if something repulsive and frightening had entered the room, voices died abruptly and heads turned to look at the invader.

Coley said, "You guys want to fight, go on and tear each other apart and bleed to death. You have a common problem, something that has nothing to do with which one of you is ethical or unethical. You don't lick this problem and it won't make much difference after the goons take over. How many of you are willing to talk to the Senator?"

Cantor said, "I talk plenty."

"Who'll back him up," Coley cried.

Matt Dennis said, "I back him up."

Weiner snorted, "Back up with what? You can't corroborate Cantor's story of his troubles, he can't corroborate yours."

Coley said, "Let the Senate counsel worry about how and who can corroborate. Meanwhile, he'll get a picture of what's going on in the Garment Center."

Weiner said, "Just a lot of character assassination, that's what it's going to amount to. Dennis is going to rip his partner apart. Innocent or guilty his partner's name will be blackened. Innocent or guilty he'll be a marked man so that people in the industry will shy away from him. Is that what we want?"

Lazetta said, "I don't like to admit it but Weiner is right. In this country we say a man is innocent until we got proof, facts that show he's guilty."

Coley pleaded, "If enough of you men tell the Senator what you do know, he will see that there is a certain similarity in your stories, a connecting link, so that all can't be dreaming up tales of gangsterism in your industry. You can bet your life he'll investigate every complaint. Every hood who ever threatened you will be picked up for questioning. From these hoods, the Senator will learn enough to get a good case started against the king-pins behind the muscle men. The main point is you've got to show the Senator there is something very wrong on Seventh Avenue. How many of you will go with Mr. Cantor to Foley Square tomorrow morning? Mr. Simpson? Mr. Lazetta?"

Lazetta said tiredly, "I told you, I got a wife and children to worry about. Most of us have the same trouble I got; we're scared green. Twelve manufacturers are asked to come to a meeting that affects every one of them. How many showed up? Six, and a representative. What happened to the other five?"

Cantor said, "Business engagements, some are sick."

"They're all sick." Lazetta said. "Sick in the gut,

like me. They stayed away because they were afraid word of this meeting would get to the organization people who are trying to push us out of the Center. They have enough trouble without looking for more. Me, I got five per cent more guts than they have, but it's a wasted five per cent."

Coley said, "You're so scared, how come you don't sell out to this Syndicate?"

Lazetta's smile seemed forced. "So help me, I don't know. I guess I got a little self-respect left. If Joe Cantor can hold out, I can too."

"Then fight them, like Joe Cantor is doing. Before it's too late, you men better stick up for your rights. Once that Senate committee goes out of existence, who you gonna holler to?"

Gross opened his mouth long enough to say, "We'll worry about it then."

Weiner said, "This cops and robber stuff is a lot of nonsense. Respectable business men want to buy in with our firms, what we supposed to do? He's got the money, he's a nice guy, we take him in. That's how it's been since Eve made Adam a partner in her apple business. Just because a guy has trouble—which he's got to blame on somebody, a human trait—he hollers crook, robber, racketeer."

Coley said, "You know what's going on, Mr. Weiner. You know this is a situation that must be forced out into the open. You know you can't dismiss it as easily as you're trying to do."

"You know so much about it, Walsh, how come?"

"I just happen to know."

"You can do better than that."

"I can't talk about it now."

"What amendment you plead?"

"What's that supposed to mean?"

"By any chance were you a part of this Syndicate, as you call it?"

Vague suspicion now rolled into cold conviction.

"You don't really want to know. You've already been briefed by Pete Carlyle, haven't you, Mr. Weiner?"

"What you talking about?"

"The man who runs this Syndicate, Pete Carlyle. How much of your business does he own, Mr. Weiner?"

"You got your goddamn nerve, ripping a man's reputation for no reason. You know so much, give us the lowdown."

"When the time comes, I'll talk plenty. Tell that to your boss."

Weiner came to his feet. "I don't have to listen to this crap. You're just wasting my time and the time of every man in this room."

Abruptly and without apology he stalked out of the room.

Simpson sighed, "Might as well go home. My wife's not feeling so good."

Matt Dennis said to Hy Croft, an elderly round-shouldered man, "Like this, you got a big mouth. Comes to a meeting, you all of a sudden get dumb."

The wisdom of his years shone in Croft's eyes. "Out of respect for my friend Cantor, I came. What's the use of talking when I know it's going to end, nothing with nothing. After all, my friend, I been in this business forty-two years. In the old days we fought goons with goons. When we won we had peace for a while ..."

Matt Dennis got up. Wearily he said, "I guess you're right, Hy."

The meeting had disintegrated into nothing, the whole thought and action now concentrated on another drink, another smoke, handshaking and a little horseplay.

Coley sighed, "We lose, Pop. The Senator was right. He got no help from industry in the union investigation. He won't get help from the dress manufacturers when and if he gets around to racketeering in the Garment Center."

Cantor said, still not believing, "In a million years who could believe a gentleman like Mr. Carlyle is a gangster ..."

## Fourteen

The elevator man helped Joseph Cantor remove his raincoat. "Kind of early today, Mr. Cantor."

Cantor turned the coat inside out, draped it over his arm, stepped inside. "Couldn't sleep. Anyway, seven-thirty is so early?"

The door slid closed noiselessly. "Don't catch me coming in before I got to. Why should I?"

Cantor watched the floors roll by. "Coming in before time is only for bosses. When is it gonna stop raining?"

"What you expect in April?"

"Rain," Cantor said.

"How's the missus?"

"Fine. Next week she'll get up and do a Kazotzki dance."

Walking down the hall, Cantor fumbled for his key.

Of course, Bessie would be all right. Hadn't the doctor said so? But right now it wasn't the same Bessie. Like a cloud blotting out the sun, shadows had formed a film over her face and hollowed her beautiful eyes. In two weeks, God willing, she would go to Miami Beach and if business permitted, he would join her for their first vacation in twenty-five years. A second honeymoon ...

Cantor had just reached the darkened double-door when the two men came out of nowhere. From out of the corner of his eye he caught a blur. Before he could turn something hard jabbed into his back, cutting off his breath.

A voice, quite muffled, said, "Don't start nothing,

Pop, or you'll be a sorry old man."

Another voice, more distinct, said, "We don't want to hurt you so don't force us. Now open the door and shut off the alarm. Then make your regular telephone call to the Protection Agency. Don't do anything you don't do every morning."

Not daring to turn, Cantor unlocked the door with trembling hands, reached up quickly to shut off the sharp ring of the burglar alarm. One of the men moved in front of Cantor to flip on the lights. Cantor gasped at the horrible face, the features long and twisted. Then he realized the man wore a lady's mesh nylon stocking over his head and face. The second man's face was less repulsive.

Both were neatly dressed, in gray raincoats. The ties were knotted just right between long white-on-white shirt collars. Their gray kid gloves were unbuttoned. Cantor could see the outlines shaped by the automatics in their shoulder holsters.

The taller man clutched a brown paper package in his left hand. "You got some new numbers, Cantor, for tonight's Charity Fashion show at the Waldorf-Astoria. You can bring them out for us."

Cantor stared, his voice a croaking and agonizing whisper, "Please, boys, I got a couple dollars in the safe. Not those dresses."

"Let him call the agency," the other man said.

"Screw the agency. Let's get finished and out of here." He tore at the brown paper exposing a metal gallon can. Cantor's eyes shrieked their anguish. "I pay you good, please."

"Shut your hole. This'll learn you to play ball." The shorter man laughed. "Maybe we oughtta wait until the models come in so they can show how those dresses look on them. Then we could pour the stuff right over their heads ..."

The tall man pushed Cantor. "Get moving, Pop, into the showroom. That's where you keep your stuff, isn't it? Just open the doors and get out of the way.

Cantor shook his head in disbelief. Tears clogged his voice. "We got to be represented in the show tonight. It's for charity. Those gowns—"

"A little cleaning don't hurt, Pop." He unscrewed the cap. "Open the doors—"

"No," Cantor cried.

"This will convince you that you shouldn't even think of running down to Foley Square."

The short man pushed open the sliding doors. "These them?"

Cantor begged. "I give you a thousand dollars, two thousand."

The tall man ignored him. "We'll give everything the business!"

"No!" Cantor slammed his fist into the man's face. "Murderer!" He shouted. "Dirty murderers! Police!"

The gun butt caught him on the side of his head, staggering him. Desperate fury distorting his face, Cantor rammed into the tall man, knocking the can out of his hands. The liquid came gurgling out of the opening, soaked into the carpet. Swearing, the short man picked up the can. Cantor came at him, hands open as if to scratch or choke. The pain caught him in the back of the head. The room rocked and spun crazily, and the floor opened in a blaze of light, dissolving into sudden darkness that opened its arms to receive him.

After a while the blackness opened like a torn veil and he could see light and hear voices murmuring around him. A moan escaping his lips, he tried to sit up but lacked the strength.

"What is it, Joseph," the familiar voice of Hershel the cutter said. "What happened?"

"Happened?" Cantor pushed himself up, the sweat breaking out in glistening rows across his forehead. The two Italian sewing-machine operators, Mrs. Santarola and her daughter, Anne, hands clasped, eyes full of unshed tears, stood huddled against the wall. "Something happened?" he said.

The acrid smell assailing his nostrils reached his brain and with a sinking feeling suddenly he remembered.

"My garments," he cried, struggling to his feet. "Where ...?"

Mrs. Santarola touched Cantor's head with her handkerchief and showed him the red stain. "Blood," she said.

"The dresses," he cried, pushing her away, staggering half way across the room to the open closet and stood staring, lips working, face gray as ashes.

How they had worked over these dresses! Sadie the designer spending hours to put on the drawing board what her mind had conceived. Hershel, the cutter, his electric machine following the pattern, grumbling as she stood over him. Mrs. Santarola, the operator, thrilled at this special job of sewing the pieces together, giving shape to pieces of rags; her daughter skillfully working on the garments with the hand needle, the final touches before Lepke the presser took over. The models, Mille, Sandra and Adrienne giving the garments life.

Then the designer had a new idea and the garments were re-cut, re-stitched and remodeled. Day and night working so that Cangro could have the outstanding creations at the Waldorf-Astoria fashion show.

But two hoodlums with a can of acid had in split seconds destroyed what had taken hundreds of hours to create.

Cantor's teeth went down tightly over his lip to keep it still and, moving in a half-daze, he went into his office. Like a man bereft of his senses, he sat and rocked in his chair.

# Fifteen

A cigarette in his mouth, Coley paced the floor of Mille's apartment in short, jerky strides. Mille, sitting on the couch, clasped her hands so tightly together the knuckles were patches of white flesh and bone.

"What'll they do next time, Coley?" she said in a whisper, not looking at him. "Those beautiful dresses, it broke my heart."

He stopped, fists clenched, aching for the chance to rip into someone. "What do you want me to do? You want me to walk into Carlyle's flat—shooting bullets? I'm pinned down in a foxhole and I can't get out to start fighting. Big strong Coley Walsh, all he can do is sit and wait and he doesn't even know for what he's waiting. That Senate committee will get around to the Garment Center in its own sweet time. Meanwhile, those goons could bury us all."

Her eyes were dry and hot. "Coley, if we could clip Carlyle's wings, what would happen? I mean, this Garment Center business you told me is Carlyle's idea. Suppose he lost his job?"

"Maybe the Syndicate would follow up his idea, maybe they'd drop it for a while. I don't know. At any rate we'd have a little time, enough until that Senate committee gets to work. But Carlyle isn't losing his job, so stop dreaming."

"I'm not dreaming, Coley, I'm planning."

He sat down on the couch to face her. There was excitement in the flush of her cheeks. "I'll lend you my gun," he said. "Next time he asks to take you out, invite him up here. I'll hold his hand while you plug him."

"We got to fight fire with fire."

"I got plenty of matches."

"What would happen if Carlyle's gambling rackets started to lose a lot of money?"

He stared in honest bewilderment. "The Syndicate

is interested in returns. Carlyle's boss, Duke Regan, would get rid of him or ship him to some other city if Carlyle couldn't carry his own weight ..." He gave her a troubled glance. "If you're thinking what I see in your eyes, it's no dice. When I was a kid I learned stool pigeons weren't people, they were dirty four-legged creatures who lived in walls and in cellars."

Her words were sharp and bitter. "No matter what you call it, if it will save Mr. Cantor, it's justifiable."

"I didn't like it when I was a kid or now."

"Isn't your attitude a little too wholesome?"

"Let's not argue about it."

"You didn't hesitate to try to convince those dress manufacturers to run to Foley Square."

"That's different. I wanted them to fight for their rights and what belongs to them. Don't you see why I couldn't spill what I know to the Senator? This isn't my headache, not really. I worked for Carlyle. I can't sing like a two-buck stoolie."

Relentlessly, she cried, "You yourself told me that when the time came you would back these manufacturers with what you know about coercion and blackmailing in the Garment Center."

Cold tension centered in his stomach. "Someday ... Maybe ... I don't know."

Her sharpness of tone belied the love in her eyes. "Is it principle that worries you, Coley, or self-preservation? You could give the Police Department a list of Carlyle's gambling establishments. You could hurt him so badly, his boss would get him out of New York. But you won't, not because you have some kind of aversion against stool pigeons, but because you're afraid you'll be implicated; you'll lose your police job."

He shook his head. "You're wrong and you know it." He rolled his shoulders to lighten the feeling of weight on his back. "If I found out about Carlyle's activities by chance or through someone else, I'd blow the whistle on him in a minute, but I worked for the guy, he trusted me—"

"Carlyle never trusted anyone. He just felt safe you'd never tell of his activities because you'd be cutting your own throat. Coley, we've got to stop him. You are our only hope, you and your knowledge of Carlyle's bookie and policy joints. You did worse things in your life."

"I'm not boasting about it."

"Then you're not going to help Pop? You and your cockeyed moral code that a pack of thieves and hoods conceived for stupid kids to swallow."

He wore a stubborn unhappy look. "Cut it out, baby, please forget it."

She moved close to him, her gaze soft on his face. "I know how you feel, Coley, but I love the Cantors so much all I can think of is saving them from the likes of Carlyle. Those poor old people ..."

"All right, all right," he said, suffering in all its tortures, in all its deadliness, the conscience pangs of an amateur stool pigeon. Averting his eyes, he said, "You've convinced me. New let me get used to the idea."

Inspector Northrop's burly frame filled the mahogany swivel chair to overflowing. Thick lips puckered, he studied the notebook paper in his hand. After a while he lifted his head and stared at Coley sitting to one side of the blue metal desk.

"This stoolie wrote these four addresses out for you?"

His lips dry despite constant wetting with his tongue, Coley looked at Inspector Northrop's shock of gray hair. "No, sir. He read off the addresses, swore they were big drops for some kind of Syndicate, and I wrote them down."

Heavy eyebrows contracted. "Did he know who runs these drops?"

"No, sir."

Shrewd eyes searched Coley's face. "Why didn't you take this list to your captain?"

Tension crept under Coley's skin. "The captain is off today, and I was afraid those addresses couldn't wait. For instance, that one-four-oh number is an all-around floating gambling game that could disappear overnight. For all I know, every one of these drops might be out of business by the time your division pounces on them."

Inspector Northrop wasn't satisfied. "Your captain is your superior. He won't like the idea of you stepping over his head."

Coley clasped his hands and leaned forward. He hadn't given the list to Captain Wentigrid because he knew what the captain's reaction would have been. "Don't mess around, you'll get your fingers chopped off." And the Captain's questions might be more embarrassing and to the point. Besides, the Captain collected a tax from two bookie joints on the list.

Coley said to Northrop, "I'm sorry. I guess I was so excited, getting those addresses, all I could think of was getting it directly to the man in charge of the division."

Still skeptical, Northrop said, "You're not the excitable type, Walsh. I should know. After all, you worked plenty jobs with me."

Coley spread his hands. "You want me to give that list to Captain Wentigrid when he returns the day after tomorrow?"

Northrop shook his head emphatically. "'Course not. I'm just trying to ascertain whether you had another reason, besides losing your head in the excitement, for going over your captain's head."

Coley blinked. "I don't understand, sir."

The inspector said brusquely, "Were you by any chance afraid there might be a leak?"

"You mean Captain Wentigrid ...?"

Northrop looked away. "Somebody ... anybody ..."

"Oh, no sir. I got excited—"

"You said that." Northrop shifted in his chair, pulled at his trousers out of his crotch. "This stoolie did work for us before?"

"Just for me. Nothing important. Crap games in the back yard, stuff like that. I once did him a favor and got Judge Kinder to give him an S.S. on a dis. con. He's been grateful ever since."

Northrop grunted. "For how much cash? And don't tell me paying off a stoolie is against departmental rules." He played with his chin as he looked over the list again. "It's amazing how these stoolies dig up information. You know this man, whoever he is, is playing with his life, if he is known to the organization or individual who runs these joints."

Coley shrugged. "I guess he knows that."

"Yet he comes running to you. ... Skip it." He pushed himself out of his chair. "I want you and Fields in on these raids."

"I've got a detail for tomorrow. There are summonses—"

"Forget them for one day." He smiled down at Coley. "You got this list and I think it only fair that you be in on the glory and the kick. Just one thing. You're not to mention this to anybody. When my boys make simultaneous raids, only you and I will know exactly where. I won't take a chance of a leak."

## Sixteen

Biting his lower lip in deep concentration, Billy slipped the screw through the two holes in the metal pieces of the erector set.

"Nut," he said sharply, imitating the doctor requesting a scalpel on the television show.

"You calling me?" Coley said from where he sat

beside the boy on the carpeted floor.

The boy laughed and said, "C'mon, Dad, this bridge is gonna fall apart."

Coley attempted to slip the nut onto the screw but Billy would have none of it. "Gimme, gimme, gimme," he cried.

"Here, don't rip my finger off."

In a moment, the nut tightened, the boy looked down at the book of picture instructions. "What next, Dad?"

Coley read the instructions, scratched his head. "This thing makes no sense. We got no more brackets."

"Who said so?" Billy said, giving his father a pitying look. "What do you call this?"

"What d'you know," Coley said, whistling in surprise. "Here, lemme hold these girders ..."

Outside the rain beat against the window like hail. Rivulets formed and ran down the pane. Thunder rolled in the distance and the rain came down faster, slapping hard.

Mom came into the room. "It's past nine o'clock, Coley. I wish you didn't have to go out in this weather."

"It's a special detail, Mom. You know that jingle about the postman? We're no different. The inspector sings and we dance, rain or shine."

Big brown eyes in a pale face looked up at Coley. "Dad, you're not gonna finish this bridge with me?"

Coley mussed up Billy's hair. "You're doing okay without me. Sorry, boy, next time maybe. Tell you what, take the set to the hospital Monday. I'll be up Tuesday, sure as shootin', I promise, word of honor, and we'll build the best bridge ever invented."

The boy, obviously disappointed, turned back to his set. "Sure, Dad. If you come Tuesday ..."

"Where you get that 'if' stuff?" He squatted to kiss the boy's cheek. "Don't forget, in bed by nine-thirty and don't raise grandma's blood pressure. Nine-thirty, on the dot ...

In the foyer closet, Coley slipped his jacket off the hanger. The afternoon papers, lying discarded on the couch screamed their big black headlines.

MILLION DOLLAR GAMBLING
RING SMASHED
53 ARRESTED

Early that afternoon Inspector Northrop and his division men had swept down on two of the four addresses supplied by Coley. Fifty-three men and women, including Henny Woods, had been arrested and booked in the station house; accounting sheets, tabulating machines and other office equipment were confiscated; the furniture and gambling apparatus had been smashed into unrecognizable pieces of wood, metal and glass.

Tonight, the third address, a floating crap game, was scheduled to be raided by a squad of division men, Inspector Northrop and Coley Walsh. The fourth address, a high-priced bordello for tired business men would be visited by the division lieutenant, three plainclothesmen and Ben Fields.

From behind him Mom said, "Coley, next time they take your picture, give the photographer a big smile. You look so serious."

Below the headlines was the picture of a wide-eyed, obviously startled Coley Walsh, carrying a typewriter to the patrol car.

Carlyle, he thought, will get a real bang out of this picture. Carlyle, alone, you can handle. But if the Syndicate backs him up, you got trouble up around your ears. Okay, so you're a cop. So the Syndicate might hesitate to get 25,000 cops on their tail by knocking you off. Then again, they might not give a damn. In the old days a cop blocking the Syndicate's progress would get a plot out in a quiet cemetery.

It would be simpler for the Syndicate to forget what you've done and start new banks, new drops in different neighborhoods. That boss of Carlyle's, what's his name, Duke Regan, is a businessman and he's got nothing personal against you, a cop who blew the whistle. But ...

He shrugged mentally as he got into the car. What was the name of that song? *Que Sera, Sera*, What will be, will be ...

The rain had slackened to a drizzle that clung to the windshield like fine mist. The wiper made a foggy half-moon. The rear view mirror showed Coley a quiet, deserted street as he shot up the block and turned the corner. One hand on the wheel, he got a cigarette out of the pack beside him on the seat, slipped it into his mouth. Reaching for the lighter, he glanced up into the mirror to see a black Chrysler bearing down on him.

Cold fingers touched his spine and ran up to his neck. The Chrysler's twin windshield wipers seemed to be working with abnormal speed. The corner street light hit the gray face flattened against the windshield. It was Henny Woods.

His cigarette falling out of his mouth, Coley hunched over the wheel, shot past the red light. With his free hand, he slipped the .38 out of the holster, lay it on the seat. The Chrysler was moving alongside now. Coley picked up the revolver.

The bus came out of nowhere. One minute Coley had all the room in the world, the next moment there wasn't a fraction of an inch to spare. The cry stuck in his throat, Coley turned the wheel, striking the bus a glancing blow. The wheel flew out of Coley's hands, the car mounting the sidewalk. A moment later a luncheonette store window opened for him in a crash of splintering wood and shattering glass. The car stopped abruptly, slamming the steering wheel into his chest with a sickening thud. The pain ran up to Coley's face and head and he had a peculiar sensation, as if he were swimming in the East River and the water was hot. Then the pain was agony.

Somebody was screaming a mile away as the darkness, cold and comfortless, closed in around him.

Coley awakened abruptly, as if a giant hand had lifted him out of the black pit into the bright sunlight. His head had a peculiar heaviness, and there was a tightness around his chest. He took a slow breath, stopped short as the pain ran down to his groin. The air was close with the odor of hospital disinfectant. A somber quiet hovered over him.

Coley didn't have to wonder why he was in the hospital. From the second he'd opened his eyes, he'd known. As if he'd awakened from a nightmare still fresh and vivid in his memory, the accident was starkly clear in his mind.

A nurse's face came into view. "What is it, Mr. Walsh?"

He blinked up at her. "I didn't call."

"You were moaning."

"This thing around my chest, it's so tight I can't breathe."

She smiled. "It's just the adhesive tape. You have three fractured ribs."

"My chest hurts, and I got a headache."

"The doctor will be back this evening. He'll prescribe something for your headache."

"A lousy aspirin and you gotta have a doctor's affidavit?"

The nurse said, "You have some visitors, Mr. Walsh. Your mother and two men are outside."

He said, "Would you send Mom in?"

When he looked around, a few moments later, his mother stood there, shy, hesitant. "Coley, oh, Coley. You're all right, Coley?"

"I'm okay, Mom. A couple days and I'll be back on

the job."

"That car. I said you didn't need a car."

"Yes, Mom, you said so. You'll see that Billy gets back to the hospital on Monday?"

Soon the conversation lagged; there was nothing more to say, no questions to ask.

"You want me to bring anything when I come tonight, Coley?"

"You can bring the papers, if you want. And, Mom?"

"Yes, Coley?"

Coley grinned. "No food packages. I don't want you and the neighbors to cook and bake for me."

When she was gone Coley closed his eyes and when he opened them two stalwart men were in the room, their faces grim. He knew before they'd displayed their shields that they were policemen.

"Kelly," the taller man said, "Police Commissioner's office. This is my partner, Benson. We just want to ask a couple questions."

The nurse said, "Do you feel all right, Mr. Walsh?"

His eyes on Kelly's swarthy face, Coley nodded. "Of course. What do you boys want?"

Benson smiled. "That car is sure a wreck."

Coley said, "Maybe I was speeding a little but it was an accident."

Benson said, "We didn't come to check up on vehicle and traffic regulations."

Coley's gaze shifted to the ceiling. "No? The Commissioner isn't checking on my health, is he?"

Kelly said, "That car was a new Caddy convertible, Walsh. It was your car, wasn't it?"

Coley said, "You could check down at the Motor Vehicle Bureau. It's mine, all right." Slow fear slurred his words. "I got a good buy."

"A $4500 car."

"I told you I got a good buy."

"What do you call a good buy, a bag of peanuts?"

"Twenty-five hundred. I can show you the bill of sale. I borrowed some money from my mother."

Benson leaned over the bed. "That load of cash in your pocket, you borrowed that too?"

The fear exploded in Coley's breast. "What you talking about?"

Kelly said, "Twenty-eight hundred and sixty dollars. You explained the car so easy, maybe you could explain the money too."

All the strength drained out of him, Coley said in a hoarse whisper, "So help me I had around sixty bucks ..."

"Some good angel dropped you a bonanza."

Coley ran his tongue over his dry lips. The atmosphere was hot, sticky, as if his head were in a hot oven, shutting off his breath.

"You guys wouldn't believe it."

The line of Benson's lips broke upon bitterness. "Every day some hungry cop gives the department a black eye."

Coley cried, "It's nothing like that."

"No sooner do we clean up one case and wipe the dirty headlines off the front page, some other bastard pops up to give us a shiv in the back."

Kelly said, "Stop getting your bowels in an uproar. Maybe he can dream up another explanation."

Benson said, "Captain Wentigrid's precinct plainclothesman."

Coley called, "Nurse!"

Benson said, "You don't have to look for protection."

"Nurse," Coley said as she came over to him, "I'm very dizzy. Maybe you could give me a pill or something."

She straightened the blanket around his chest. "The doctor will be here soon ... I think you've had too many visitors."

Kelly said, "Sure, nurse. Walsh, we'll be back

tomorrow with the police doctor. If he says you're fit, you'll fill out one of them questionnaires. When you do, we'll be able to work on you. Maybe we'll clear you, maybe not."

Benson held up a set of keys. "They're yours," he said, lips twisted in a smile. Dropping the keys on the metal table, he left, his partner at his heels.

Coley reached over his shoulder but a stab of pain arrested his motion.

The nurse said, "May I help you?"

"Give me those keys on the table."

He tore them out of her grasp, held them over his eyes, thumbed each key out of the way. In a burst of anger, he flung the ring from him.

The bank vault key was missing.

They had him over a barrel now; they knew it, he knew it. Tomorrow when Doc Nardiello, the police doctor, examined him, Coley'd be told he was in good enough physical condition to fill out a questionnaire, and swear to it under oath. Then they would have him in the soup. Just sign the questionnaire, Walsh, go on, sign it; the statements you make as to your assets, how you obtained them, how you got the money to furnish your apartment, swear they're true.

You wouldn't be the first cop heaved out of the department for committing the crime of perjury.

The Syndicate had played it cute. For twenty-eight hundred dollars, insurance money, they had guaranteed that if Coley Walsh didn't die in the accident, at least he'd be heaved out of the department. Then he'd be just another guy in the street, a lot safer to tackle.

Coley lay there for a long while, his eyes burning with the fever of hopelessness, then he sat up, pulled at the blanket. The room began to spin as he dangled his legs over the bed. He dug his hands into the blankets, held tightly until the walls eased back into place. Big drops of perspiration formed at his hairline as he worked his legs down slowly, carefully. For a second he thought the floor was coming up to meet him as his toes touched the cold floor. A drop of sweat rolled down his nose. He took a step, dropped to his hands and knees.

The pain around his chest was dull at first, sharpening into agony as he crawled toward the clothes closet. Grasping the door knob, he pulled himself up, opened the door, a sob of relief escaping his lips when he saw his clothes hanging neatly on hooks and hangers.

The nurse came into the room, all her professional dignity gone when she saw him. "Mr. Walsh, what are you doing out of bed? You are not to leave the bed for any reason, including the bathroom. Those are Dr. Levin's orders." She slipped a gray and black-striped robe over his shoulders. "I'll help you back into bed."

Coley shook his head so hard the sweat came off in a fine spray. "After I make a telephone call. Will you please get the change out of my coat pocket?"

"You are not going out of this room."

"Don't make book on it, sweetie."

"Perhaps I could make the call for you."

"This is too personal. Will you get the change? Or did the police grab that too?" Coley chewed on his lips, for the pain had come again, sharp, numbing. "Just a couple of dimes."

"I shouldn't do this." She stepped into the closet and when she came out, laid six dimes and seven quarters on the dresser.

Coley picked up two dimes. "Where's the telephone?"

"This is in your responsibility." She pointed, "Across the hall. Let me help you ..."

"No." His breath was coming in short gasps. "You'll get in a jam if they catch you helping me to a telephone. Don't worry, I'll make it on one leg."

Holding his breath, Coley moved stiffly with his

back straight out of the room across the cold floor, into the telephone booth. He sat down quickly, his stomach heaving and turning. He tried to wipe the mist out of his eyes and succeeded to the extent that he could dial the operator. His elbow on the supporting platform, Coley held the phone tightly against his ear. Sweat flowed freely, his eyes smarting.

To the operator he said, "Police Headquarters."

When the brass voice of the switchboard man answered, Coley gave him the number of the precinct. The phone rang twice before a singing voice answered.

Coley said, "Amelia, Coley Walsh. Is Captain Wentigrid in yet? Yeh, yeh, I'm okay. You guys sure get news fast. What about the Captain? What's his home telephone? Of course, it's important. You think I wanna get my tail chewed off?" He blew sweat off his lips. "Wadsworth two-one-oh-. Thanks, pal ... I don't know. I'll send you a copy of my hospital chart."

Amelia was still asking questions when Coley pulled down the hook with his free hand. As he put the second dime into the slot, he wondered why he hadn't given the operator his badge number so that, this being an official call, she could return his dime. Thinking about it he began to laugh. Imagine worrying about dimes when his whole life was at stake! What could you expect from a guy in fever?

Slowly, biting his lip, he dialed Captain Wentigrid's home number. Almost immediately the receiver lifted at the other end.

"Captain Wentigrid, please. Oh, it's you, Captain. This is Coley Walsh ... Yeh, I feel pretty good. Captain, I'm in trouble. I need your help."

Captain Wentigrid's voice was hale and hearty. "Oh, it can't be too bad. If it's the civil suit you're worried about, you can make an out-of-court settlement for the damaged store front." Coley shook his head, tried to talk, but Captain Wentigrid's voice was loud in his ear. "As for the speeding and dangerous driving charges, we might be able to clear those up."

"Will you let me talk?" He paused for breath. "Captain, two men from the Police Commissioner's office were in to see me a while ago. Tomorrow, they want me to fill out a questionnaire. You've got to stop them."

The Captain said, "Is that all? Tomorrow, you go right ahead and fill out the questionnaire. You've got nothing to hide. You have no assets, I'm sure, no real estate, no big bank account and no bank vault. Do I make myself clear?"

Coley moaned. "Sure, Captain, but I don't seem to make myself very clear. I crashed in my own car, a Caddy convertible I'd bought for two thousand and five hundred dollars."

"You damn fool."

"Also, they found two thousand and eight hundred dollars in my pocket. It wasn't mine, but when you got about ten grand in a vault, the twenty-eight small bills don't matter. Yeh, they took my vault key. When I answer my questionnaire, how do I explain those things, Captain ... Hello? Captain ...?"

Captain Wentigrid sounded tired. "Where does that leave me?"

There was a hard, suffocating feeling in Coley's chest. "I'm coming right over to straighten this out."

Wentigrid said, "Don't come here. I'll be in the precinct."

The phone dropped out of Coley's hand, dangled. He pushed himself up, made his way back to his room on rubber legs.

The nurse hurried over. "You must get back into bed."

Coley stood staring at her, fighting the weakness rising in him. "Who the hell you giving orders to? Get out before I heave you out."

Stiffening, the nurse said, "I'll be back with the

doctor. Meanwhile, I'd suggest you get into bed before you collapse."

Coley watched her flounce out of the room. That had been pretty easy. Getting dressed would be something else again. The sweat broke out again as he opened the closet door, swept his clothes from the hangers.

"Coley? What's this?" Mille stood in the doorway, gray eyes wide with amazement.

"Mille! God, I'm glad to see you." He dropped his clothing on the bed. "Help me to get dressed."

"I will not ..."

The sweat ran into his eyes, burning. "Mille, I got no time to argue. I must get to my precinct. My job depends on it, my life. Mille, for as long as I need it, I've got to hold onto that job. You gonna just stand there?"

## Seventeen

A gray and murky low ceiling had settled over the city. The air was humid and uncomfortably warm. In the taxicab Coley stretched out his legs to ease the tiredness in his thighs. Mille wiped his face with a handkerchief.

"You shouldn't be out, you're sick."

"You don't know how sick I'm gonna be if my captain can't help me." The taxicab drew up in front of the precinct. "Pay the hackie, like a good girl."

The weariness had sharpened into pain. Angrily, he closed his mind to it as he moved up the short stairs to the precinct doors.

"I'll help you." Mille took his arm.

He tried to focus his eyes on her. Her vision faded for an instant, blurred, returned sharp and beautiful.

"I love you, honey," he murmured. "But I got to do it alone. Wait for me ..."

Mouth open, the desk sergeant's eyes followed

Coley across the floor to the captain's door. Once, fearing Coley was falling, he came off his chair, then settled back when Coley straightened out and opened the door.

Ben Fields was waiting for Coley on the other side of the door. Solicitously, he took Coley's arm.

"When I saw you banged up this morning I would have bet my wife against a dime you wouldn't walk for a month."

Coley eased into the chair to face Captain Wentigrid. "I had to get out of the hospital," Coley said. "That's all there was to it. I got a problem. How we gonna solve it?"

Captain Wentigrid's face was flat, emotionless. "I wish I could help you, Walsh. But I'm tied up, literally, figuratively, my hands, my feet, mouth, like a damned mummy."

Coley swallowed the lump in his throat. "Maybe you could reach somebody, Captain, somebody who could get the P.C.O. men off my back. They got me good, and all the fairy stories I can dream up won't get me off the hook ... unless you can put in a fix."

Wentigrid said tiredly, "Only the Commissioner himself can call off those men."

Fields' eyes were erratic. "You sure got yourself into a jam. And you've dragged us in with you. All your goddamn fault. Don't tell me different. You were too damn smart. You know what you done to us, Coley?"

Coley said apologetically, "I suppose it wouldn't make any difference to tell you I was framed on that money found in the car? I guess not. Like that case you had, Ben, where the guy was convicted of burglary in Queens, when all the time he was innocent because he couldn't tell the court his alibi; he'd been pulling a payroll job in Manhattan."

Captain Wentigrid leaned on the desk. "Now that you're on the carpet, the P.C.O. will, sure as hell, turn their light on Fields and me. They'd have to." He sighed wearily and slumped in his chair. "Part of the blame is mine. I should have got you transferred long ago. There were too many rumors of you and that Syndicate. Your hands were in too many pies. Then that business over in Brooklyn, killing the man in that Cantor's house. I wanted to get rid of you when I heard you were sticking your nose into that Garment Center, having talks at Foley Square that was none of your damn business. Don't look so surprised; word gets around."

Fields said, "I was for getting you broke back to a beat. Nothing personal, Coley, but I knew sooner or later something like this would happen. I wanted the captain and me should protect ourselves."

"Why didn't you, then?"

Fields chewed violently on his lips for a few seconds. "We couldn't, not after you made the front pages on that Cantor case." Bitterness crept into his tone. "You were a big hero. How would it have looked if all of a sudden the captain got you out of this precinct?" An unintelligible curse came sobbingly out of his mouth. "Coley, you son of a bitch, I told you to get away from the Syndicate. I told you to get rid of that car."

"You told me," Coley said. "How does that help now?"

"I wish I'd known," Wentigrid cried. "We wouldn't have to be tearing our hair out now." His chin almost touched his chest. "I've got a lot of years in this department. In the twilight of my career."

A lock of hair, wet with sweat, dropped limply over Coley's forehead. "You got more years left, Captain. Lift that phone and start calling every politician, every big shot you know."

"It's no good."

"What the hell can you lose?"

"I already have made calls. It's no use."

Coley sat stupefied for a few moments. "So that's how it is. What's my status now, Captain?"

"You're under suspension on Inspector Northrop's orders. You'll turn in your equipment."

"Anything I can do ...?" Coley laughed harshly. "That's a joke. What can a broken cop do? If I could fight this ... if I had a chance."

Fields said, "You got no chance, Coley, but we have. You fight this and you get yourself a front page trial. Maybe you get a kick out of seeing your puss on the front page. Lately your publicity has been all right. But those black, dirty headlines may not look so good to your family. And the department will get another black eye. I suppose I got no right to talk about things like that."

"Get to the point," Coley cried.

"Resign," Fields said, "and the P.C.O. men might not dig further. The captain and me might not get involved."

Captain Wentigrid said sadly, "You're deluding yourself, Fields. They've got their foot in our door, they'll come all the way in."

Fields' lips were dry and flecked with cigarette tobacco. "A prayer, I still got a prayer if Coley resigns."

Coley rubbed his eyes with his knuckles. "Captain, do me a favor? Get me up a letter of resignation. Send it over to the hospital so I can sign it." He dropped his badge on the desk. "My revolver is over at the hospital. I'll hand it to the guy you send over with that resignation letter. If you'll get somebody to go over to my house, my mom will give him my spare revolver."

Captain Wentigrid didn't seem to be listening. "Tomorrow, I'll hit them with my retirement papers. If they refuse to allow me to get out on a pension, I'll fight them."

Fields watched Coley make his way to the door. "Can I help you back to the hospital, Coley?"

His lips twisted into a smile. "You want to push me under a truck, don't you?"

Fields nodded. "In a minute, if it'd do any good. But it's done ..."

Coley said, "Thanks, Ben ... Oh, I'll be all right."

As he went out the desk sergeant called after him. Coley didn't look back. The station house was no longer his second home. The men in it were no longer his brother officers. This would be the last time he'd ever set foot in here again.

Outside, Mille took his arm.

## Eighteen

May started off cool, wintry, but sunny, compensating for the week of rain that sent April into history. Coley had been home now for three days. After removing most of the adhesive tape, the doctor had advised Coley to rest for at least another week.

The silk robe wrapped snugly around him, Coley welcomed Mille and Joseph Cantor.

"Hi, doll. Not you, Pop, her." He kissed her twice. "Thanks for the basket, Pop." Coley nodded in the direction of the cellophane-wrapped fruit and candy basket standing in the corner. "Mom, please get the bottles and stuff."

Mille said morosely, "Sure, let's celebrate."

Clothes baggy, eyes bloodshot, Cantor looked very old and very tired. As the man drank, his hand shook, some of the whiskey dribbling off his lips.

Coley said softly, "They're still at it, aren't they, Pop?"

The skin under Cantor's jaw was suddenly slack. "No more. Since yesterday they don't bother me. No more acid, no more trucks smashed, no more crazy telephone calls four o'clock in the morning." His eyes bulged. "They are not wonderful people?"

Coley said to Mille, "You explain it, maybe it'll

make more sense." He took the highball glass from Mom. "The way Pop talks, he sounds like he's sold out to them."

Mille looked at Pop, pity and compassion in her eyes. "What could he do? Even iron can be made to bend. Monday, Mr. Carlyle is coming up to the office to sign a contract."

Cantor laughed shortly. "It's out in the open now. I mean that Mr. Carlyle feller. I talk to him direct. I know you, mister, I tell him, so don't hide behind a high hat. What you want I give you so stop the telephone calls which are making my wife a nervous wreck."

"A little while longer, Pop, a week, two. I've been thinking how we can chop his head off."

Cantor shook his head violently. "Enough! Look at you! You should see my Bessie. Remember how she used to walk, tall and proud? Now she's got fright in her eyes. She don't walk so straight anymore. Who needs it? Before they kill somebody, before my Bessie dies from aggravation, I give up. Coley, my son, it's better like this."

The sourness of defeat was tight in Coley's throat. "They beat us, after all. Carlyle and his damn hoods."

Cantor stared glassily at Coley's feet. "Now I can go to Florida with my Bessie. Now I can live without worrying what's gonna happen tomorrow. A old man like me, one foot in the grave, should quit working. Maybe I sell out the whole business to Mr. Carlyle. Who needs the lousy business?"

"Sure, Pop," Coley said. "You're right one hundred per cent."

The business was Cantor's life, Coley knew, and a man like Cantor couldn't just step out of the hustle and bustle and excitement of the Garment Center and live a life of ease on the sands of Miami Beach, not without shortening his life.

Coley said, "Anyway, you don't have to worry

about my fifteen per cent, Pop."

"Oh, no." Cantor said. "I sell, you get a piece also. Fool, what I gonna do with money? And when you and Mille get married, I'll still make you a big wedding, if God spares us."

Coley looked at Mille. "We should have been married a long time ago, Pop. But I was a dopey guy. One month, Pop, just give me thirty days to get a job and I'll ask Mille if she's still willing."

Mille came to him, kissed him gently. "Mille always was and always will be willing."

Cantor said, "Pick out a wedding present, something good."

Coley pressed her hand in his, then leaned back in his chair. "For a wedding present I'd like Carlyle's head on a platter."

Mille sat on the chair arm, her hand on Coley's shoulder. "I could give it to you before the wedding. He asked me out for Friday night. Nerve? He's got plenty. I told him off about Mr. Cantor and it didn't bother him one bit. Suppose I accept his invitation, then we could go for a ride in the country and I could plug him full of holes and you could meet me and we'd bury him ..."

"Cut it out," he said.

She sighed "It did sound good."

"I, too, figured out a plan," Coley said. "I could beat the daylights out of him and get his written confession, and the police would put him away for life. Like in the movies. But in real life, that confession would never stand up in court because he could say I obtained it by threat, torture and banging his head against the wall. No, I'd need more evidence. Then I got another idea ..."

He moved to the edge of the chair "Pop, maybe we could still pull it off. Pop, will you give it one more try? You can get Carlyle to make statements that would be better than a confession."

Cantor frowned. "Enough trouble. What's the use?"

Coley clutched his glass tightly. "Suppose Carlyle makes statements of his own free will about how he tried to beat you down, Pop. Suppose he also makes a couple of threats. Suppose he shoots off his mouth and we get it all on a tape recorder."

Cantor didn't seem to be listening. "Trouble, all the time trouble."

Coley heaved himself off the chair. "Pop, listen to me. It's a long shot but it's worth a try. I once worked on a wire-tap job. We got complete data on a high-priced call house. The words were recorded nice and clear, every voice so recognizable we had no trouble connecting it up with each and every girl who used the phone. Pop, we could wire your office."

Mille said, "Carlyle is too smart to make incriminating statements, not unless you can get him off guard."

Coley pointed to Cantor. "That's Pop's job. Up in Cangro's Carlyle'd be off guard. Look at Pop. Does he look like the type who'd pull a tape job? Who'd suspect him? And you got to remember Carlyle will be feeling real good when he goes up there with his lawyers, a respectable business man buying into a business. Okay, he comes in. Pop is alone, no lawyer, nobody. Carlyle is annoyed. Where's Pop's mouthpiece? Then Pop hits him between the eyes; Pop's changed his mind. He's still not sure he wants to sell. Can't you see Carlyle blowing his top? Hell, he's not a cake of ice. He can get excited and swear and curse. Pop can pull it off. A couple wisecracks, and when Carlyle's steaming, bang! Pop talks about the hoods hounding him, the attack on his wife, the acid, the damages, the whole business down on the tape. And, I'll bet my life, Carlyle will give enough admissions and enough threats to give us something to work on."

Breathlessly, Mille said, "It might work."

He heard a sound and looked up to see Pop working his lips as if something displeased him.

"Pop, it can't miss."

"Who am I, Paul Muni? I can't act. Anyway, I don't want it."

"We got to fight poison with poison. It's all we got left."

"It's not for me."

"You just wanna give up and die?"

"Thinking about such a thing makes me sick. I know I don't do it right and if Mr. Carlyle finds out who knows what he'll do. No, Coley. It's not for me. For my Bessie's sake, for your sake ..."

"Don't worry about me. I can handle myself."

Cantor sighed. "I can see by your bandages how you can handle yourself. I'm sorry. That I didn't mean."

"Pop, one more try, one more fight."

Cantor got up, black misery etched in every line of his face. "My Bessie wants I should sell the business. She is frightened and I can't blame her. When Mr. Carlyle comes Monday, I give him a good proposition ..."

Abruptly he went to the doorway. Over his shoulders, he said, "Once and for all, I live in peace ..."

Cantor was gone and it was quiet for a long while. Forlorn and depressed, Mille still sat on the arm of Coley's chair. Coley got up, walked to the window and stared into space. Even when her soft sobs broke the silence, he did not turn.

"Monday," he said, "I'll go out and get a job. I got a couple contacts. One guy owns a flock of movie houses ... then we'll get married."

When she didn't answer, he turned to stare at her profile and as he watched he saw tension and an inner excitement mounting in her.

"Take it easy," he said.

"Coley." She moved swiftly to his side and slipped one arm around his waist. "Those recorders come in pocket-size, don't they?"

With his fingers his wiped the tears under her eyes. "Let's forget about recorders."

Her eyes were big and luminous. "Peter is very fond of me."

"I know what you're driving at; I don't want any part of it."

"With me he's relaxed and off guard."

"No."

"I can do it, Coley."

"No."

There was determination in the set of her jaw. "With your help or without it, Coley, I'm going to try to trap Carlyle. For Pop, for us, for our whole future, I've got to make the attempt."

He moved away from her to the cigarettes on the table. "You don't know what you're up against. Maybe Carlyle will fall for it, chances are he's too smart. What kind of excuse you got for going out with him all of a sudden when you've been refusing his invitations?"

There was no mirth in her smile. "I had a fight with you, we broke off and I'm very lonesome. He'll believe me because he's in love with me."

He felt a jealous pang. "I'm not interested. Don't you see, doll, it won't work. Maybe you'll get something on him, and maybe the recorder will be deemed illegal and inadmissible in a court of law. But what bothers me most is that it's too dangerous."

She took the cigarette out of his mouth. "What can we lose, Coley? You said that yourself." She blew smoke. "Coley?"

He took her hand, kissed it. "I got everything to lose—you. You're wonderful, but I can't take the chance of jeopardizing your life because your life is my life and why should I commit suicide?"

She returned the cigarette to his mouth. "Suppose Peter did catch on to what I was doing? I could laugh it off. He wouldn't believe it was funny but all he could do is walk out on me."

"I can't take the chance."

Gray eyes blazed in her flushed face. "Friday, I won't see you, Coley. I will have a date with Carlyle." There was confidence in her tone. "I can do it. The telephone book should be full of places that sell recorders. I'm sure a set of instructions go with every purchased machine."

"I could call up Carlyle and kill your plan."

She kissed him and a tear brushed onto his face. "Don't you see, Coley, I must go ahead with it."

The breath came out of him in a long drawn out whistle. "Okay, you win. Let's not cry about it now. There's a place on Church Street that sells small pushbutton recorders."

## Nineteen

A gigantic doorman dressed in a Cossack uniform opened Carlyle's car door and stepped aside. Mille came out, a tiny hat on the back of her head matching her blue silk shantung suit. Under her arm she clutched a navy blue handbag. Carlyle, neatly dressed in a charcoal-gray business suit, looked like a typical man of distinction as he tipped the doorman and ordered Henny Woods, sitting beside the chauffeur, to park and wait somewhere down the street.

The moon was a full, yellowish ball in a starlit sky. It was comfortably cool.

Allen Street was not Broadway but it was a lively street. Gowned women and tuxedo-clad men joined those in more conventional garb in a trip down the five steps to the restaurant.

Carlyle stepped back from the car. Woods glanced

at Mille, his eyes cold and distrustful. The chauffeur, Bandy, a squarely-built man with large ears, pulled away from the curb, and the car rolled down the cobblestoned street.

Mille held her bag tightly against her, then, remembering Coley's instructions, kept it nonchalantly but firmly at her side. There was nothing in her bag but a compact, a handkerchief, the twenty-seven-ounce recorder and, connected to the machine, a microphone smaller than a half dollar. A piece of fitted cardboard separated the machine from the microphone so that the microphone could lie snugly between the torn lining and cloth. Carefully Coley had scraped away at the cloth where the microphone would rest, leaving only a thin film of material. Now, he had no doubt, the voices could be clearly recorded.

The restaurant was a mysterious world full of candlelight and music, the atmosphere smelling of seductive perfumes. Glittering women and suave men sat whispering around the tables, seemingly oblivious to the orchestra playing Hungarian music.

Excusing herself, Mille went to the ladies room where she powdered her nose and applied fresh lipstick. How to get Carlyle to discuss Cantor was her problem. Once, in the car, Cantor's name had come into the conversation. The recorder hadn't been operating. What Mille had wanted was to broach the subject, hoping to pick up the thread in the restaurant. To have the recorder operating from the time she'd left home would be taking too much of a chance: The recording wire would run for two hours maximum.

"Figure it to run ninety minutes," Coley had instructed. "Just to make sure. You got a lousy hour and a half to outsmart the weasel."

In the car, Carlyle had barely talked about Cantor and the Garment Center. Instead, he had told her about the furnishings he would get for a house he was building in Scarsdale, and boasted about a neat piece of stock manipulation that had doubled the purchase price.

In the mirror, Mille straightened her dress, fixed a silver earring. The matron was busy with a buxom woman who had had too much wine. Mille opened her handbag. The rectangular yellow recorder stared up at her, the four pushbuttons like ivories on a piano. The time indicator at the zero line, Mille pressed the pushbutton marked RECORD. The ready-light blinked on and inside the machine, the recording wire began spinning wire faster than a foot a second.

After checking the microphone inside the lining, she snapped shut her bag.

The orchestra was playing a Hungarian rhapsody which had an intoxicating, aching throb. She slipped onto the chair the waiter held out for her. Carlyle ordered wine and in a few minutes the waiter was pouring a dark red liquid into goblets.

Carlyle said, "It's a Malaga wine, heavy and sweet."

She looked bored. "Oh, that's good."

He drank some wine, then refilled his glass. "You're not drinking, Mille."

The handbag seemed hot and heavy on her thighs, the side containing the microphone facing in Carlyle's direction. "I don't know what we're celebrating."

"Just us, you and me and the music. Isn't that enough?"

"I suppose so." She sipped wine.

A man, tall as a reed, a red sash around his middle, glided out to the center of the floor. Slipping a violin under his chin, he lifted the bow high, and began to play.

Carlyle said, "When Tamaroff plays I feel icicles moving up and down my back. It's gypsy music, although actually I don't believe the gypsies create original music. Rather, they travel from country to country, Russia, Hungary, Rumania, and they pick up these tunes and make their own arrangements."

Deliberately not answering, Mille fixed her gaze on the handsome woman, elbows on the table, hands holding up her head, ample breasts supported by the table.

Carlyle took Mille's hand. "What's the matter, darling?" His voice was soft, almost pleading. "You got Coley on your mind?"

She laughed. "Of course not. The last one in the world I'd want here just now is Coley Walsh."

He seemed happy. "Somehow I believe you really mean that. You know how I feel about you, Mille?"

She watched the violin player move from table to table. "You like attractive women walking down a restaurant aisle with you."

Hurt narrowed his eyes. "That kind of woman I can get for a twenty-dollar bill. You must know I love you, Mille."

"Do you, Peter? How much do you love me?"

He looked puzzled. "How do you measure love? I want you to be my wife, Mille. Is that love enough? Marry me, Mille?"

She stared at nothing. "I couldn't marry you, Peter."

"You don't love me."

"I like you very much, Peter."

"We're back to Coley Walsh."

"You are, but I wasn't even thinking of him. Do you know, Peter, Coley hasn't even got a job? Oh, but you do know."

He grinned, new confidence in his manner. "I figured a good job could make a lot of difference. Oh, no offense, Mille. A girl has to be weak in the head to marry a bum when she can get somebody who can supply her with everything she could ever want. And I make a lot of money, Mille."

She laughed. "If money is the basis of a good marriage I could do better marrying your boss, whoever he is. He does make more money than you, doesn't he, Peter?"

He lifted his glass. "You wouldn't like Duke Regan. He's too fat, too old and too cold."

"But he makes a lot of money."

"Yes. Someday that money will be going in my direction."

The violinist was at their table, his head bobbing as his nimble fingers moved up and down the board, the bow jumping.

Mille said, "You have promotions in your organization like a civil service job where you take an examination ..."

He said, "The man with the strongest men backing him is sure to come out on top of the promotion list." He squeezed her hand. "I can't talk about it ... but I'll be on top a lot sooner than some people think."

She held her glass up. "We'll drink to it."

They clicked glasses and he said, "To my plans, Mille, drink to them. Two months and you will marry one of the three biggest men in the country."

The violinist backed to the front of the restaurant, stopping for a bow.

Carlyle said, "Will you marry me in two months, Mille?"

"Don't I get time to think it over?"

He laughed happily. "Of course. Twenty-four hours. That's as long as I can wait. We'll live like royalty, Mille. The money will come rolling in from all sides. You can't imagine how much ..."

Mille said, "There must be a thousand ways you boys have of making money."

"We're businessmen with good investments."

"Oh, come now, Peter," she gave him her brightest smile. "You're a lot smarter than the man who just buys and sells for dollars. You're smart enough not to have to gamble by investing."

She saw the gleam of watchfulness in his eyes and

knew he would not be susceptible to her patronizing.

He said, "Why don't we just drop the subject and eat. In fact, darling, let's forget everything except you and me and my proposal."

The waiter bowed, and after Carlyle had ordered roast beef for Mille, goulash for himself and another bottle of wine, moved away on noiseless feet. A dark-haired girl came out amid thunderous applause and when she began to sing a hush fell over the house. Carlyle seemed content to sit and listen.

Impatient, knowing the recorder was spinning away precious feet of wire, Mille said, "I've thought it over, Peter."

He turned. "You thought ...?"

"Your proposal, Peter."

"Oh, I'm sorry. Bella has such a wonderful contralto voice—"

"I don't think I'd be happy with you, Peter."

The singer forgotten, his body came all the way around. "Why do you say that?"

Her gaze was direct. "Joseph Cantor."

Annoyance flickered over his face. "What's he got to do with us?"

"You must know how I feel about Mr. Cantor. Peter, he's like a father to me."

There was an odd mixture of anger and perplexity in his eyes. "How come that Cantor always manages to get into the act? I've heard all I'm going to about that guy."

"Peter, I must talk about him, if we're going to get married. I've got to get things straight in my mind. Why did you do those things to the nicest man in the world?" She hesitated, fearing she was overacting. "You're responsible for everything that's happened to Mr. Cantor."

Nostrils flared. "I'm having a meeting with Cantor and his lawyer on Monday. We'll sign papers and be partners. So you can invite the old man to our wedding."

"You didn't answer my question."

"I don't intend to."

"The attempts on his life, the hijacking of his trucks—"

"Would you rather go home?"

She sighed deeply. "I—I'm sorry, I was carried away. But I do love Mr. Cantor and if I married you my conscience would plague me for the rest of my life."

Calmly, he said, "Some more wine, Mille?"

After a while the waiter brought their food. Mille toyed with her roast beef, her mind in a turmoil as it desperately sought a way of inducing Carlyle to implicate himself. She glanced up to find him staring at her, a smile on his face.

He said, "You've lost your appetite, I'm afraid. And it's all my fault."

She pushed aside the plate. "I was just thinking you're going to have trouble with Mr. Cantor as a partner."

The smile faded. "I don't think so."

"Mr. Cantor is one hundred per cent honest. Now I know you businessmen have clever ways of saving a lot of money."

"For instance?"

"Oh, you must know ways, Peter, to beat the government."

"You mean income taxes?"

"I'll bet you're too clever to get caught."

"I am too clever to cheat."

"Oh come now, Peter. You must have smart accountants who can keep two sets of books. You're not a stupid man, Peter."

He shoved his plate to one side, put both elbows on the table. "I don't understand you." His forehead was a mass of fine lines. "You've never talked this way before. It doesn't sound like you, and all these questions ..." His eyes were bright, nostrils quivering. "And I don't like it."

She thought. You're just an amateur up against a major leaguer. Forget trying to outsmart him and go home.

"Maybe it's the wine," she said. "I feel so light-headed."

He seemed satisfied. "Let's dance."

She shook her head. Twenty-five minutes had vanished since she'd set the wheels in operation, and she'd accomplished nothing. She had to make more attempts to unlock the business thoughts he kept locked in some hidden compartment securely separated from his private life.

"Not now, Peter ... after Monday's meeting—"

"Enough talk about that."

She hesitated, then decided she had no choice, said, "Just one question, Peter. Suppose you and Mr. Cantor don't agree on the terms of the contract? Suppose Mr. Cantor changed his mind about taking in a new partner?"

The muscles along his jawbone rippled. He picked up the wine glass, set it down. "He won't change his mind because he asked me to join him and I'm sure your Mr. Cantor doesn't welch even on oral agreements."

The words came out sharp and mocking. "Suppose he welches on you. What could you do about it?"

"Nothing."

"You wouldn't hurt him or his wife, like you've already done."

"You didn't drink that much wine."

"Would you send hoods to throw acid on his dresses like the last time?"

"Let's get out of here, Mille."

"You've got to answer me, Peter. I've got to know for my own peace of mind. You did hijack Cangro trucks—"

"You're getting hysterical."

"Admit it, Peter, admit it."

"I never hurt Cantor in any way."

"Not you personally. But you sent your men to do your work."

Carlyle signaled the waiter for the check. "I'll take you home. Perhaps we can have a drink over at your place."

She bowed her head, trying desperately to keep the tears from overflowing, knowing she had lost the battle of wits. Clutching her bag, anxious to get into the car with Carlyle, hoping and praying she would have one more chance, she almost tripped over her own feet.

"Easy," Carlyle signed the check, returned it to the waiter. "I guess it was the wine after all." He chuckled. "I was beginning to think crazy things. Guess I'm too suspicious at times."

They went up the steps to the corridor leading to the lounge just as a man was coming down. The big man's lips were flecked with spittle, the eyelids heavy with alcohol. Mille tried to get out of his way but he brushed against her, knocking her against Carlyle. The handbag fell out of her hand to the carpeted floor.

Carlyle pushed the drunk so hard he went stumbling into the dining room, barely missing one table, before finally crashing into another.

Carlyle turned to Mille. "You all right?"

She nodded, then remembering, looked about her. "My bag."

As Carlyle swept the bag off the floor it upended and the recorder dangled in the air by its yellow cord. Mille gasped, cold and shaken, as Carlyle opened the bag wide. Wordlessly, no surmise in his face, Carlyle pressed the STOP button on the recorder, pushed the machine into the handbag, and snapped it closed. The whole episode from the time the drunk had knocked into Mille had taken split seconds.

Two waiters were helping the drunk to his feet. The manager came bowing to Carlyle.

"I must apologize for that man. I am terribly sorry …"

Carlyle's face was a stiff mask. "That's all right, Boris. Give the man a bottle of wine, charge it to me. My compliments. Come, darling," he took her arm. "Let's get out in the fresh air."

She moved to the corridor and in a dead voice, said, "Please give me my bag."

His softness of tone could not hide the sharp anger. "I should have known. Perhaps I did way back in my mind, but I had a mental block. We'll talk it over in my house."

A voice that sent thrills of relief through Mille said, "We can talk it over right here."

Carlyle started, turned just as Coley yanked the bag out of his grasp. Coley said, "Don't start anything here, Pete."

People stopped to look for a second, then passed on.

Carlyle, whispering hoarsely, said, "Give it to me."

Coley pushed down the outstretched hand. "You can have it, after we make a deal."

"I'll cut your heart out for this business."

Coley touched Mille's band in a gesture of reassurance. "Not here, you won't. You start anything and the cops will come and this recording will be in the public domain. When that happens nothing you or I can do will keep your business quiet. This way, maybe we can make a deal."

He moved down the corridor away from the people arriving and departing.

Mille shook her head. Coley didn't understand. There could be no deal because she had failed miserably.

Coley stopped short of the men's room, quickly ran his hands down Carlyle's body. "I didn't figure you carried anything ... What do y'say, Pete, you wanna play it my way or you want to sing for those two buzzards you got out in the car? It's your decision because you know what's in this recording, I don't."

"There's nothing in it," he said hoarsely, "not a damn thing."

Coley didn't look at Mille, slipping a cigarette between his teeth, he said, "Then what are you so sore about? If we got nothing, it's a joke that didn't come off."

"Give me the recorder and we'll forget the whole thing."

Mille said tiredly, "Give it to him, Coley. It won't help us."

Coley frowned. "He's too anxious."

Carlyle chewed on his lower lip. "I could get you another job in the organization, Coley."

Coley said carelessly, "In exchange for the recorder."

"Of course. It's no good to you ..."

"I'm not so sure about that, Pete."

"Five grand for that box."

"Can't use it."

"Ten grand and my promise I'll forget what happened tonight."

Coley's eyes widened. "Well, what d'you know. For a lousy unimportant recording, you sure want to pay a fancy price. I don't want your money, Pete; this is not blackmail, I want a deal, something simple: Lay off Cantor and Cangro's. That's all."

Carlyle's eyes were sick. "That's all? You don't know what you're asking. Name a price, any price ..."

"I already named a price."

Two men came out of the men's room and, puffing on big cigars, went by. Another man entered the men's room.

Carlyle mopped his face with a pocket handkerchief. "If I say okay, I won't touch Cantor, will you give me the goddamn contraption?"

Coley shook his head. "You must be kidding. I'll put the recording where you can't get your hands on it. As long as there is peace and quiet at Cangro's, nobody but you, Mille and I will know it exists. In a year or so, when I feel Cantor is safe, I'll ship it to you."

Carlyle clenched his fists. "In one day you could make a dozen duplicate recordings. All my life I'd have this thing dangling over my head."

"Maybe stand on the corner and sell them like newspapers. H'ya, get your latest wire recording … Pete, you'll just have to take my word that when I send you the roll of wire it will be the only one in existence."

"I can't do it."

Coley shrugged. "So long, Pete. See you around."

Carlyle clutched his arm. "If I get jammed up a lot of people are going to suffer. You, Mille, the Cantors. I'll get my revenge one way or another." His face was distorted with fury. "I'll kill you, every damn one of you."

Coley said, "You sound like a lousy movie."

"Last chance, Coley."

"Tonight this will be in the hands of the police, after I hear what's given you the shakes. I hope there's enough in here to get the F.B.I. on your neck."

Carlyle backed up two steps, turned on his heel and ran for the street door. Fear skimmed across Mille's widened eyes. Coley took her arm, steered her toward the dressing room.

"We got to get away before Carlyle gets to those hoods. There must be a back alley. Never knew a restaurant kitchen that didn't have one."

Side-stepping tables, almost upsetting a waiter, they weaved their way across the dining room to the kitchen. The chef and his helpers turned to stare, mouths open. Coley saw the door. "C'mon, baby, get the lead out."

A waiter with a tray went flying to one side as Coley went around a table, yelling out an apology. The chef picked up a chopper, swung it over his head, jabbering something in a foreign tongue, but not coming any closer to Coley.

"You, too," Coley said.

Now they were in the narrow alley. Before he could become accustomed to the semi-darkness, Coley slammed into a garbage can. The noise was deafening, reverberating between the yellow brick walls. Mille's handbag in one hand, her wrist clasped firmly in his other, Coley stopped at the mouth of the alley and looked out.

People strolled up and down the street. The Cossack doorman was opening the door of a taxicab. Half a block away Carlyle, Woods and the chauffeur were hurrying to the restaurant. Carlyle said something to Henny Woods, and hurried down the steps, with Bandy, the chauffeur, a step behind him. Woods stepped back to the curb, hands at his side, on the alert.

Mille cried, "Give them the recorder. It's no good to us."

"It must have something to freeze Carlyle's eyeballs."

"I don't understand it."

Coley pointed. "I got a hired car parked across the street. It's a nineteen fifty-five blue and gray Dodge convertible. You can see it, the one behind the maroon job."

She nodded. "Parked in front of the poultry store."

"Walk out of here, nice and easy, cross the gutter and get the car started. Here are the keys. You'll have your back to Woods and he won't be looking for a girl alone. I got no time to talk about it. In a minute Pete and that chauffeur will trace us right through that alley."

Lips tightly clenched to stop the quivering, Mille

took the keys and, with bated breath, at Coley's signal, walked out of the alley, mingling with the strollers. Coley flattened himself against the wall, his eyes fixed on the kitchen door ten yards behind him. He took a quick look at Mille crossing the gutter. His gaze shifted to Woods, back to Mille. But she was out of sight now.

Coley stared down at the handbag as if it were something strange and alien. Why hadn't he given it to Mille!

The alley door opened with such suddenness it hit against the brick wall. Carlyle and his chauffeur came running, stopping short when they saw Coley.

Carlyle gave a loud, exultant howl. "Gotcha, Coley, you no good bastard."

With a quick motion Coley lifted the garbage can, flung it at them. He didn't wait to see what damage he'd done. In two quick strides he was out on the sidewalk, sidestepped a woman and raced across the gutter. A truck missed him by inches, the driver sticking his head out to tell Coley exactly what he thought.

Mille had the door open. Coley flung himself into the car, slid behind the wheel, reached out to close the door. Carlyle and Bandy were racing toward him. While Carlyle was momentarily blocked by a car, Bandy kept coming.

"They'll shoot us," Mille cried, "and for what? A worthless recording ..."

"They won't shoot." He sucked in air. "Too many witnesses around and there's a cop on the corner." Coley could see Carlyle's sweaty face as the car jumped away from the curb. Bandy swore at him. The car took the corner on two wheels. On the next block, Coley slowed down.

"All we need now," he said, "is to get stopped for a ticket. Maybe we lost them. They had to go back for the car and that would take time." Block after block went by and no Cadillac showed in the rear-view mirror. "Yep, we beat 'em for the while. Oh, oh."

Mile looked up into the mirror, a frightened look in her eyes. "How did they find us so quickly?"

Alerted at once, Coley hunched over the wheel. "Woods went for the car when Carlyle and the chauffeur came after us."

Coley made the Battery in a long sweep and turned into the West Side Highway. Every few minutes the Cadillac vanished from view, only like an ogre in a nightmare, to come out from behind a car. At Ninety-sixth Street, Coley decided at the last moment to chance the streets again. He twisted the wheel, shot down the incline, passed a red light. The mirror showed no Cadillac behind them.

"Keep your fingers crossed," he said. "They went past the exit and it'll take them a while to straighten out. They're sure to try a U turn and I hope to hell there's a cop up there watching."

## Twenty

It was past midnight when Coley rolled the car down a dirt road, stopping in front of a lake shimmering glassily in the moonlight. The breeze, cool and soft, ruffled the dark lake. On either side of them black trees were silhouetted against the sky.

Coley shut off the motor, leaned back in the car, his breath coming out in a long drawn-out sigh of relief. "Okay," he said "Let's get on with the séance now."

Mille took the recorder out of the handbag, squeezed the pushbutton marked REWIND.

They waited, somewhat impatiently. Coley said, "We could have done that an hour ago. It's supposed to rewind around five times faster than its forward speed. You think it ran an hour?"

"Less. Cigarette, Coley?"

He lighted cigarettes and they waited in silence

while the minutes ticked away. Ten minutes later Mille checked.

"It's ready," she said quietly, plugging the microphone into the playback socket. Chewing on her lips, she squeezed the pushbutton marked PLAYBACK. Heads almost touching, Coley held the microphone between their ears.

First there was the sound of Carlyle's voice as she had come out of the ladies' room, then came varied voices, loud, soft, brassy, muted, as they had made their way to the table. A chair scraped, music played, thin and metallic. Carlyle's resonant voice, easily recognizable as he rolled his r's like a boy in a speech class, ordered the wine from the waiter.

Carlyle: It's a Malaga wine, heavy and sweet.

Mille: Oh, that's good.

Mille said to Coley, "It doesn't sound like me."

Coley laughed. "Because you don't know how your voice sounds."

Carlyle: What's the matter, darling? You got Coley on your mind?

Mille: Of course not. The last one in the world I'd want here just now is Coley Walsh.

Coley chuckled. "How true, how true. I can hear a fiddle. He use a bow or a back-scratcher?"

"He played a beautiful gypsy song."

Coley perked up when Carlyle said: I want you to be my wife, Mille. Is that love enough? Marry me, Mille?

Mille: I couldn't marry you, Peter.

Coley said, "That's my girl."

"Quiet," Mille said. "Listen to us tear you apart."

"I'm listening."

Carlyle: A girl has to be weak in the head to marry a bum when she can get somebody who can supply her with everything she could ever want. And I make a lot of money.

Mille: If money is the basis of a good marriage I

could do better marrying your boss, whoever he is. He does make more money than you, doesn't he, Peter?

Coley growled. "That fiddle player is getting into the act."

Carlyle: You wouldn't like Duke Regan ...

Now the violin playing was loud in the microphone, drowning out the conversation. Coley swore, shook the microphone.

Mille said, "I tried to get Peter to talk about his money, how he and Regan made it, how they cheat the government out of income taxes ... anything to get a case against Carlyle and his Syndicate. I failed, Coley, and that violin player had nothing to do with it."

"Let's listen ... The fiddler is gone."

With one hand, Coley took two cigarettes out of the pack, slipped one into Mille's mouth, one between his own lips. The lighter flicked on. Coley sucked on his cigarette, blew smoke angrily.

"That guy is too shrewd to fall in a trap."

The microphone registered applause, then seconds later, above the orchestration, could be heard a contralto singing. Mille's voice sounded very strained as she talked to Carlyle about a proposal she could not accept unless she knew what part Carlyle had in the acts of violence on Joseph Cantor, his wife, his business.

Coley stirred in his seat as Carlyle fended off her questions.

Mille: You're going to have trouble with Mr. Cantor as a partner.

Carlyle: I don't think so.

Mille: Mr. Cantor is one hundred per cent honest. Now I know you businessmen have clever ways of saving a lot of money.

Carlyle: For instance?

Mille: Oh you know ways, Peter, to beat the government.

Carlyle: You mean income taxes?

Mille: I'll bet you're too clever to get caught.

Carlyle: I'm too clever to cheat.

Mille said to Coley, "He's clever in more ways than one."

Coley sighed, "He's been around, it isn't easy catching him off guard."

Mille: Suppose you and Mr. Cantor don't agree on the terms of the contract? Suppose Mr. Cantor changed his mind about taking in a new partner?

Carlyle: He won't change his mind because he asked me to join him and I'm sure your Mr. Cantor doesn't welch even on oral agreements.

Mille: Suppose he does welch on you? What could you do about it?

Carlyle: Nothing.

Coley said to Mille, "What did you expect him to say?"

Mille tossed her head. "I'm sorry. I tried."

He kissed her cheek. "I'm not blaming you. Nobody could have done better."

He listened to Carlyle ordering the check, then telling Mille he would take her home where they could have a drink.

Carlyle: I guess it was the wine after all ...

"I stumbled," she explained. "Now we're going through the dining room, up the stairs ... Now!"

The sound of the recorder hitting the floor was loud and dull.

Carlyle: You all right?

Mille: My bag.

A few moments later the microphone was dead.

Sighing, Coley pressed the STOP button. "Nothing," he said, a note of sadness in his voice, "not a damn thing. I don't get it. Was Carlyle so loaded he thinks he might have said something?"

She said, "He wasn't drunk in any sense of the word. Perhaps that's where I made my mistake. I should have taken him up to my apartment, fed him liquor till it came out of his ears."

He smiled faintly. "Not Carlyle; he's too smart to drink that much. He can't be a lush and stay where he is up in the Syndicate. Is there anything you remember that Carlyle said that could hook him in any way?"

She pondered the question. "I don't think he said anything that would send me running to the police."

"That part where the fiddle player comes in loud and clear, what were you talking about?"

She watched him light two cigarettes in his mouth. Taking one, she said, "Nothing important ... oh, yes, it was about Duke Regan."

He stirred, new interest in his voice. "Regan? How did he get into the conversation? Wait a minute, let me play the beginning over again. You get in the mood and concentrate, please, with all your mind. This could be it!"

While the recording wire was rewound onto the original spool, Coley went out of the car to smoke his cigarette. There was a chill in the air now. He picked up his coat collar but the cool air fingered his body through his clothing. Idly, he wondered if he were getting a cold, then laughed at himself. Worrying about a cold when his life and Mille's were at stake! If Carlyle and his senior delinquents ever caught up to him, a cold would be the least of his headaches.

"Okay," Mille said, "it's ready to roll."

They listened, tense and quiet.

Mille: I could do better marrying your boss, whoever he is. He does make more money than you, doesn't he, Peter?

Carlyle: You wouldn't like Duke Regan.

When the violin playing came in, Coley pressed the STOP button. "Okay, what was said next?"

She mused, "I was just groping. I wanted Peter to talk about money ... Oh, I remember." Her eyes were glowing in the semi-darkness. "He called Regan old and fat."

"That's not a capital offense. Think, Mille, think!"

"I'm trying to. I said something about Regan making a lot of money and Peter said someday that money would be going in his direction."

"Go on."

"He said, I'll be on top a lot sooner than some people think."

"Now it's beginning to make sense. Anything else?"

She rubbed her forehead with her thumb and forefinger. "We drank a toast. Oh, yes, we drank to Peter's plans. In two months, perhaps he said three, I don't know. Anyway, he said I'd be married to one of the three biggest men in the country."

"Then what?"

"That's all. Coley, I don't understand."

Jubilant, he kissed her. "You're a doll. I wonder if Duke Regan knows he's slated to be thrown in the garbage can—or maybe placed in a cement block and dropped in the river—when Carlyle takes over. That's the conversation that's got Carlyle shaking in his pants. He's got a plot brewing only he evidently needs more time. If Regan should get wind of it, Carlyle'd have to run out of the country."

"But why did he tell me that?"

"Just a guy off guard, boasting to his girl. Anyway, you see, there was nothing you could do even if you wanted to. Your story would be laughed at. But this recording is something else again. Carlyle's own voice ..."

She cried, "Coley, are you crazy? What voice? What recording? That violin player ruined the whole thing. Oh, I'll never listen to another gypsy violin player as long as I live. I don't know what you're so happy about."

"This," he held up the recorder. "You and I know it isn't worth a damn. But Carlyle doesn't."

He opened the case, lifted out the two reels of wire,

stepped out of the car to fling them into the lake.

He chuckled as he pushed the recorder into the glove compartment. "This I got to return to get my deposit back."

Mille said, "I still don't understand. All right, you're going to bluff Carlyle. Good. In fact, it doesn't make too much difference if we have the recording or not." A thought penetrated. "You don't want Carlyle to find those reels."

He chuckled, "If Carlyle ever got his hands on that recording, we'd be stiffed in. It'll do us more good where it is now. As far as Carlyle knows we got him in a box."

Her voice was a whisper. "He can't stay in the box."

Coley shrugged. "He's got a choice—use a blackjack or kid gloves."

"Pick your choice and place your bets."

He frowned. "I wouldn't like to bet on my choice. I'm praying Carlyle stays away from Cantor. But if I were in his place, I'd try to grab that spool of wire ... Tonight."

Mille shuddered, raised her arm to clasp each shoulder. "Let's go home, Coley. I feel sick."

He slid behind the wheel, started the car. "That's where we can't go, baby, not tonight anyway. I said Carlyle must get that wire tonight. Tomorrow will be too late as far as he's concerned because one, we could make copies; and two, we could hide it where he'd never find it." He stuck his head out of the window and backed the car up the dirt road onto the concrete. "We stay away from him tonight and we'll win."

"Where'll we go?"

He looked at her in feigned amazement. "A million hotels in the country and you're asking where we'll go!"

## Twenty-One

It was two o'clock in the morning when they stopped in the diner for a sandwich and coffee. In a half hour, they'd be in the heart of Manhattan where Coley could put the car in a parking lot and find a hotel for the night. After picking up two packs of cigarettes, they left the diner. For the first time he noticed the gas station barely ten yards away.

Coley said, "Might as well get gas now."

He stopped short. Pulled up close to the gas pump was a familiar black Cadillac.

An ominous feeling crawling up his spine, he grasped Mille's arm. "That Carlyle's car?"

"I don't know. It looks like it. Oh, there must be a thousand black Cadillacs that look alike. If I could see the license plates ..."

He decided. "I'm not taking chances. Let's get out of here."

They reached Coley's hired car and Coley's hand was on the door handle when Woods' gravel voice said, "It's a small country, Coley."

Coley cried, "How the hell did you ever find us?"

"Luck," Carlyle said, coming from around the car. "Luck and perseverance. We were on your tail until we got to the state road, then we lost you."

Woods crowed. "Told you we shouldn't give up, to just keep moving along this road." He ran his hands up and down Coley's body. "He's clean. The big cop hasn't got his toy pistol anymore; he hadda turn it in with his tin potsy." Pushing Coley savagely, he cried, "Get in the car. Pete, I'll ride with them. You and Bandy follow us in the Caddy. Okay?"

Carlyle nodded. "Stop at the first clearing down the road."

Woods held a black revolver in his fist. "Start moving, Coley, and believe me, I'd like nothing better than to have you make a break for it."

A mile down the road, Woods ordered Coley to turn into a dirt road. The car rocked as it rolled down the incline and stopped in a partial clearing. A squirrel, disturbed as Coley stepped from the car, scooted out of a bush and ran up an apple tree.

Carlyle came out of the Cadillac, parked a few yards behind them. "Search his car. I want that recording machine. Rip that car apart if you have to."

In a minute Bandy's shrill voice sounded loud in the still night air. "Got it! Thought he could beat Pete Carlyle, the dumb cluck."

Grinning in deep satisfaction, Carlyle took the recorder. Genuinely regretful, he said to Mille, "That was a lousy trick you pulled. For that, and the fact that you got a big mouth and might say something you shouldn't, I got to slap you down good. Coley I'll cripple so he can't even walk out of here on his own legs."

Coley said, "You'll never get the recording that way."

Carlyle snapped open the box. His head came around stiffly. "Where are the reels, Coley?"

Coley lighted a cigarette. "What did you say about crippling me?"

Carlyle slapped the cigarette out of Coley's mouth. "Damn you, where is that recording?"

"Where you'll never get it. Let's talk about Cantor."

"I'll kill you, Walsh, so help me, God. I'll cut you into little pieces."

Coley said softly, "Send your boys home, Pete, and let's make talk."

Carlyle spat dryly. "With you I don't talk. That reel's got to be around here someplace. Bandy, search the car. Henny, frisk them good." He slipped a revolver out of his coat pocket. "Make it a good search."

Woods laughed. "I'll try not to rip her panties."

Coley said to Woods, "Lay a hand on her and I'll kick you right between the legs, gun or no gun."

Woods sneered, "Big mouth you got, Walsh."

Bandy was in Coley's car ripping up the seat cushions with a big switchblade knife. He came out of the car and pulled up the motor hood.

"No good," he said. "Give me the keys to the trunk compartment."

Woods took the keys out of Coley's pocket, flipped them. "I got an idea you'll find nothing in the car." Carefully, he searched Coley from head to toes and, satisfied, turned to Mille. "You're next, baby. This I'm gonna enjoy."

She flinched and backed away as Woods approached her. Coley grasped Woods' arms, turned him around. Right hand clenched, he brought it around in a hook but the blow never landed. Suddenly the sky came down on his head, exploding into a million dirty stars.

He came to with a start, as if he had overslept and was late for work. There was a pounding in his head, like steel hammers beating against a nerve.

He heard Carlyle saying, "Mille, I wish I could turn back the clock. Maybe things would be different now. I don't know. I should have killed that cop long ago. That I do know. He's got the luck of a drunk. Nine guys out of ten would have died in that car wreck. This time his luck ran out ..."

There were tears in Mille's voice. "A few hours ago you loved me enough to marry me."

Carlyle's voice was sad and tired. "That was a few hours ago. My life depends on that recording. Give it up, Mille, and you and Coley can walk out of here."

Coley pushed himself erect. "You can't let us go now, Pete. You couldn't take the chance that we'd sing."

Carlyle laughed indulgently. "Go on and talk, see

if I give a damn. It's that recording I want, nothing else."

Coley held his head in his hands to ease the throb. "Let Mille go, and I'll whisper the hiding place in your ear one hour after she goes off in my car."

"No," Carlyle said stiffly. "Henny, let's get it over with. Mille first."

Woods ran a tongue over his lips. "I don't like killing a dame," he said sincerely. "But ..." He took a breath, held Mille with one hand, lifted the revolver muzzle with the other. "Here goes nothing."

"Wait a minute," Coley cried.

"Make it fast," Carlyle cried, "No crap."

Woods was breathing heavily. "C'mon, c'mon, for God's sake."

Coley said, "You don't have to worry about that recording, Pete. I dumped it in a lake a couple miles from here."

Carlyle shouted angrily, "Don't give me that."

Mille was trembling from head to foot. Any second, she was sure her legs would buckle under her.

Her voice shook. "It's true, Peter. The recording didn't come off. Remember that gypsy violinist at our table when we were discussing your Duke Regan? The music filled the microphone, drowning us out."

Carlyle said, "How'd you know I was interested in what I said about Regan?"

"C'mon, Pete," Coley cried. "Who's playing now? There was nothing in that recording except a lot of garbage. I figured it wasn't worth a dime if you got your hands on it so I ditched it, figuring I could bluff you into playing ball."

Woods said, "You can't believe a word he says."

"It's true," Mille said.

Carlyle shook his head slowly. "I can't afford to gamble. Wherever it's hid it can stay there for the next generation to discover, and if somebody found it now he wouldn't know what it was, what it contained, who the voices belonged to, and wouldn't give a damn. Only we know what it's about and just you two know where the damn reels are, so I'm going to play it safe by burying you both with your secret. Mille, I'm honestly and truly sorry."

The sigh came from between Coley's teeth in a whistle. This was the way it had to be. He'd known that from the beginning. Appeals would fall on deaf ears. Carlyle was right. He had to protect himself.

Coley said, "You talked me into it, Pete. I'll show you where we buried the reels in a tin container."

Woods growled. "He's stalling for time."

Carlyle nodded. "I know. But there is a chance that he is telling the truth this time, and I'd feel a lot better if I had my hands on that recording. Take us to it, Coley. I don't want to visit Canada."

In Carlyle's car they rode around for a while, Coley asking them to stop occasionally so he could examine the terrain. Mille followed his movements with anxious eyes, wondering how soon he would make his play.

Woods kept needling Carlyle. "How much longer we gonna listen to this guy? If he can't find it, nobody else will, so let's get going like you planned."

Coley said, "It's around here some place. Give me a while longer."

"Ten minutes," Carlyle said, enjoying the game, "that's all you got."

The car crawled. Abruptly, Coley pointed to a dirt road. "Down there. That's the spot."

"We'll walk," Carlyle said, getting out of the car. "Henny, there's a shovel in the trunk. We'll need it, one way or another, because this is the last stop. You'll find a flashlight in the glove compartment. Bandy, you stay here in the car. Henny and I'll handle them."

They walked down the dirt road, Coley followed by Mille, Woods and Carlyle. Coley stopped before a stream where the ground was so soft his shoes sank almost to his ankles. The moonlight filtered through the canopy of trees in white eerie colors.

Carlyle looked down at his soiled shoes. "Well, Coley?"

Coley pointed to a tree, "Over there."

Woods flung the shovel at his feet. "Go on and dig. I'm betting you come up with nothing but worms." He stood over Coley, revolver pointed at him, the flashlight forming a gray cone. "Dig, you bastard, dig deep so we can bury you here. That earth hasn't been touched in a year."

The shovel bit into the soft earth. Coley looked up at Mille. Abruptly she turned and began to run up the road. Carlyle cried out.

Woods lifted his revolver, aimed it. "Now, boss?"

Carlyle said, "I had enough playing around. Give it to her."

The shovel of sand caught Woods in the face, blinding him. Before he could turn around, Coley crashed into him in a vicious tackle, the revolver dropping at Woods' feet. The flashlight flew off in Carlyle's direction. A cry of satisfaction in his throat, Coley pounced on the black revolver. Carlyle's gun jumped, the bullet catching Coley in the right side, turning him half way around. Off in the distance, the echo rolled like a clap of thunder. Coley dropped to his knees. Carlyle, crouching, moved toward him. Coley pumped two bullets in his direction, and backed away. Carlyle stood there as if paralyzed, took a half-step. Coley's third shot caught him between the eyes. He fell and rolled into the gray cone made by the flashlight. The hole in his forehead was a black quarter.

A gnomish figure came slithering down the road. The earth jumped at Coley's feet. The shovel in his hand, Woods moved toward Coley and from the side Bandy began to close in. Coley emptied his revolver, flung it into Woods' face. The man stumbled as Coley, clutching the hole in his side, stepped into the icy stream, crossed it, tripped on a rock. He heard sounds behind him, twigs breaking, the crunch of shoes on dryer land. Coley ran until the breath was gone from his body. The pain in his side was now unbearable. Exhausted, he sank to the ground.

When Coley awoke the rain had stopped, and gray dawn hung wet and misty around him. His clothes were soggy with rain, the hole in his side a hot poker. Shivering, he got up, stumbled forward, dropped to his hands and knees, fought his way up again. By yards, feet, inches, he moved through the rough terrain, and suddenly the trees opened up and he stood on the highway.

Two cars made deliberately wide turns and passed on, then a red and white convertible shot around the curb, headed for the swaying figure in the road, braked to a stop. Coley saw the round-faced man with the sports cap behind the wheel, the redheaded woman, eyes full of fright and horror. Abruptly, his legs gave way.

When he regained consciousness, he could hear voices around him, all trying to talk at once.

Then Mille's voice, sweet and reassuring, reached him. "He's lost a lot of blood. We've got to get him to a hospital."

"Don't worry, lady, he'll be all right."

Coley opened his eyes. Mille and a state trooper looked down at him.

Coley smiled as she threw her arms around him. Quite calmly, he said, "You betcha life I'll be all right."

THE END

Jack Karney was born in 1911 in New York City on the Lower East Side, where many of his novels are set. Though he tried out for a job in the police department, due to an excessive case of flat feet, he was rejected and entered the civil service instead, working in the New York District Attorney's office. Here he listened to  the trials and tribulations of cops, both veterans and rookies, and this wealth of information plus his childhood memories provided material for his many novels. Karney was married with three children, and spent his entire life in the same New York City neighborhood.

# Jack Karney Bibliography
## (1911-?)

**Novels:**

There Goes Shorty Higgins (Morrow, 1945; Pyramid, 1953)

The Ragged Edge (Morrow, 1946; Pyramid, 1951, revised as Tough Town)

Cop (Henry Holt, 1951; Pocket, 1952)

Knock 'Em Dead (Ace Double, 1955)

Work of Darkness (Putnam, 1956; Popular Library, 1958)

Cry, Brother, Cry (Popular Library, 1959)

Cut Me In (Pyramid, 1959)

The Knave of Diamonds (Ace Double, 1959)

Some Like it Tough (Monarch, 1959)

Layout for Murder (Berkley Medallion, 1960)

Yield to the Night (Monarch, 1960)

**Short Stories:**

Shake Well and Kill (*Black Mask*, Nov 1946)

**As Mike Skelly**

Halo for a Heel (Red Seal, 1952)

# Black Gat Books

**Black Gat Books** is a new line of mass market paperbacks introduced in 2015 by Stark House Press. New titles appear every three months, featuring the best in crime fiction reprints. Each book is size to 4.25" x 7", just like they used to be, and priced at $9.99. Collect them all.

**1** Haven for the Damned
by Harry Whittington
978-1-933586-75-5

**2** Eddie's World
by Charlie Stella
978-1-933586-76-2

**3** Stranger at Home
by Leigh Brackett writing as
George Sanders
978-1-933586-78-6

**4** The Persian Cat
by John Flagg
978-1933586-90-8

**5** Only the Wicked
by Gary Phillips
978-1-933586-93-9

**6** Felony Tank
by Malcolm Braly
978-1-933586-91-5

**7** The Girl on the Bestseller List
by Vin Packer
978-1-933586-98-4

**8** She Got What She Wanted
by Orrie Hitt
978-1-944520-04-5

**9** The Woman on the Roof
by Helen Nielsen
978-1-944520-13-7

**10** Angel's Flight
by Lou Cameron
978-1-944520-18-2

**11** The Affair of Lady
Westcott's Lost Ruby /
The Case of the Unseen
Assassin by Gary Lovisi
978-1-944520-22-9

**12** The Last Notch
by Arnold Hano
978-1-944520-31-1

**13** Never Say No to a Killer
by Clifton Adams
978-1-944520-36-6

**14** The Men from the Boys
by Ed Lacy
978-1-944520-46-5

**15** Frenzy of Evil
by Henry Kane
978-1-944520-53-3

**16** You'll Get Yours
by William Ard
978-1-944520-54-0

**17** End of the Line
by Dolores & Bert
Hitchens
978-1-9445205-7

**18** Frantic
by Noël Calef
978-1-944520-66-3

**19** The Hoods Take Over
by Ovid Demaris
978-1-944520-73-1

**20** Madball
by Fredric Brown
978-1-944520-74-8

**21** Stool Pigeon
by Louis Malley
978-1-944520-81-6

**22** The Living End
by Frank Kane
978-1-944520-81-6

**23** My Old Man's Badge
by Ferguson Findley
978-1-9445208-78-3

**24** Tears Are For Angels
by Paul Connelly
978-1-944520-92-2

**25** Two Names for Death
by E. P. Fenwick
978-195147301-3

**26** Dead Wrong
by Lorenz Heller
978-1951473-03-7

**27** Little Sister
by Robert Martin
978-1951473075

**Stark House Press**
1315 H Street, Eureka, CA 95501 707-498-3135
griffinskye3@sbcglobal.net  www.starkhousepress.com
Available from your local bookstore or direct from the
publisher.